FINDING REFUGE

CHRISTINE GAEL

1

FALLYN

After years of inhaling smoke and smog in Chicago, the fresh ocean air of coastal Maine was intoxicating. Fallyn breathed deep, relishing the salt spray as the fishing boat bounced gently over the waves. For the first time in a very long time, she felt fully awake and glad to be alive.

The breeze was cool, but Fallyn was snug and warm in the thickest wetsuit that the scuba shop had to offer. The thick neoprene left her feeling as bloated and clumsy as a seal, but, like a seal, she would be graceful enough underwater.

At the thought of finally scuba diving in the Gulf of Maine, her whole body thrummed with adrenaline. Excitement, for once, instead of anxiety or fear. She hadn't felt this kind of purely positive exhilaration in years.

This was the right decision, no matter the outcome.

"This is the spot," Gabe said. It was just the two of them on the boat. There were no dive tours in Bluebird Bay. She'd had to rent her equipment from a place in Waterville and then book afternoons with a local guy who usually did fishing tours.

He was younger than she'd expected, and tired under the eyes. But he was steadier than most men his age, and happy despite his exhaustion. When they had first set out, Gabe had gushed about his new baby girl.

"We named her Grace," he'd said with a mix of pride and wonder, "but everyone calls her Gracie. I loved her even before I ever saw her. Just feeling her dance inside her mama's belly was amazing. Even though we're not sleeping much, this is the best thing that ever happened to me. She makes me feel whole. Like what I do every day matters, you know? Because it's for her."

Now, though, he wore a look of skeptical amusement.

"You do know that the water's colder now than it is in *January*? It's probably not even forty degrees today."

Fallyn flashed him a smile. "I am aware. I come prepared."

She tucked her hair behind her ears and pulled on the neoprene wetsuit hood that she'd rented, then zipped her wetsuit up over it. She already had thick booties on the inside of her fins, and now she worked thick neoprene gloves over her hands and down past her wrists.

Gabe watched with interest as she prepared her mask with a layer of anti-fog gel on the inside, then donned her vest and its heavy metal tank full of air.

Fallyn had worked hard for this moment. Weeks of classes, months of research. She'd even done ice water plunges, submerging herself in a bathtub full of ice-studded water to help prepare her body for these dives. There had been unexpected side benefits to those freezing baths; Fallyn slept better on the nights she did them, and had fewer nightmares.

This little quest of hers had given Fallyn a goal when she'd needed it most.

It had saved her.

When she left her job at the Chicago Tribune six months before, she could barely function. She had seen countless horrors in her years of investigative journalism, especially when she found herself niched into covering murders and other violent crimes, but that final case broke her.

The way the man had mangled those little bodies... it was far too gruesome to print.

It was something that no one should have to witness.

And yet, Fallyn had sought it out. She had chased it down, just one more story for her portfolio... and she had regretted that decision every day since. She had promised herself that she would never deliberately subject herself to seeing an atrocity like that ever again.

What sort of masochists deliberately subjected themselves to scenes like that, day after day?

If it didn't drive her mad, it would rob her of her humanity.

She didn't *want* to be the kind of person who could look at a dead child and feel nothing.

But she didn't want to subject herself to that degree of pain anymore, either.

She had been toying with the idea of quitting for a long time. But she had kept going, because it was all she knew. It was her career. Honestly, it had been her whole life — successful and miserable, just like everyone around her. She didn't know how to break away.

And then that last story had pushed her over the edge.

For a long time, she barely left her bed. She wasn't sure she wanted to live in a world where things like that happened every day. She just didn't see the point anymore.

Her whole life had revolved around her job. She was always chasing that next story, angling for some interview or another. And when she quit all of a sudden, she had nothing to fall back on.

No hobbies. No friends. Not even a dog.

She had plenty of savings to coast on for a long time. All that winter, she hardly left her apartment. She ordered takeout and watched old movies and scrolled aimlessly through social media.

And slept.

Mostly, she slept.

It was a sort of hibernation. A long winter's rest. But eventually, after countless hours of listlessly wandering the internet, a mystery had snagged her attention. Not another gruesome murder or a grisly crime. But something new and novel, something that revived the girl she used to be.

And she hadn't told a soul. Her father, still an active journalist at sixty-six, was bitterly disappointed that she had quit her successful career. Her mother, who always sided with her husband over her daughters, had basically stopped talking to her.

She hadn't even told her sister; Nadine was too pragmatic to share her excitement. She would tell Fallyn that this was the kind of adventure that a twenty year old might throw themselves into — that it was a ridiculous pastime for a (formerly) successful woman who was nearly forty. And since her relentless pursuit of her career her entire adult life had left her with a long list of contacts and zero close friends, she hadn't had anyone else to talk to.

She had just spent months talking to herself, questioning her own sanity.

Fallyn looked up from the mask she held and met Gabe's eyes. He had an open, honest face — and he was clearly a good person. When she had booked through his website and accidentally overpaid him by sixty dollars, he had returned it to her in cash the moment she arrived that afternoon.

Maybe she was being naive. She had no way of knowing whether Gabe would blab her secret around town. But the desire to tell *someone* filled her chest to bursting.

She grinned uncertainly at him. "Want to know what I'm doing out here?"

"Are you kidding?" Gabe said. He didn't even try to play it coy. "I've been dying to ask ever since you booked a *dive* for this time of year. Actually, a bunch of dives. And with specific coordinates, no less."

She reached into her bag with one hand, clumsy in its thick neoprene glove, and pulled out a map. She handed it over. "I'm hunting for treasure."

"That was my first thought, but honestly, I dismissed it. Usually hunts come with tons of high tech equipment and a whole team..." Gabe took the map from her hand.

"Yeah, it's probably pie in the sky and all, but I figured, what the heck? I came across that news story about the pirate ship they found in Cape Cod last year. Remember that? They found the ship, but not the treasure it was supposed to have sunk with."

"Yeah, I remember hearing about that."

"Well, I kept digging—digging is kinda my thing—I even

made a trip to the museum there last month, and then to a local archive where I got access to some old logs and journals from that time period."

"How did you manage that?" Gabe asked.

"I told them I was writing a book. Which wasn't exactly a lie — I *do* want to write a book, if I can find what I'm looking for. Maybe. Anyway, multiple sources mention an altercation with another ship in the days before that famous pirate ship sank. And since that ship never showed up with the treasure either, I'm wondering if it was lost during the fight. Or if they just dropped it overboard out of spite when they realized they were outgunned."

Gabe looked out over the gray-blue water. "And you think that happened here."

"*Something* happened here," Fallyn replied. "There are multiple accounts of some sort of altercation that happened in this area. And yes, I've found enough hints pointing to the lost pirate ship to — well, for me, to go diving in forty-degree water."

Gabe chuckled. "I can't believe I'm hosting a real live treasure hunter."

Fallyn grinned at him. "When I was still in school, studying journalism, I wrote a piece about treasure hunting in the Atlantic. I always loved the idea of an ocean filled with enough riches to change the world. Just sitting there, waiting.

"These days, it's like you said. Most successful treasure hunters have tons of gear and gadgets, huge financial backing... but every once in a while, a lone hunter armed with nothing more than a map and a dream finds gold. Like in a storybook." She shrugged. "I don't know if it will pan out, but that's okay. The hunt itself has given me a new lease on life. I have enough savings that I can coast for a while, and I'm tired of being pragmatic. I want to do something that's just for *me*."

Gabe nodded and gestured out towards the horizon. "I'm a big fan of living your dream. My dad was pissed that I didn't pursue something more lucrative than this, but it makes me happy. I think my soul would shrivel up if I had to work inside an office building every day." He frowned and looked away. "It doesn't seem to have done him much good either. He got his beach house and his fancy car... but he seems miserable half the time." Looking back at Fallyn, he continued, "I think the people who value experiences over money are the lucky ones."

"Wise words. I'm obviously not in it for the cash, or else I wouldn't go telling a stranger all about my plans — even if the stranger is a kind one who hands out unsolicited refunds."

"I won't tell a soul." Gabe crossed his heart.

Fallyn actually believed him. "Thank you. I appreciate that."

"Good luck," Gabe said. "I'm excited to see what you find."

She fitted her mask snuggly over her face and sat on the edge of the boat. In one hand, she held a tiny digital camera on a stick, designed for underwater videography. With her other hand, she fit the regulator in her mouth and took a deep breath, testing it. Then, she let the weight of her tanks pull her backwards into the water.

The icy splash drove every thought from her mind. But she came to her senses a moment later. After that initial shock, the cold wasn't overwhelming. Just invigorating.

Frigid water seeped down her back, like a snowball dropped down her shirt.

I'm from Chicago, she blustered silently. *I can handle the cold.*

She kicked vigorously, moving so she wouldn't freeze. The water was deep here and she swam horizontally; she would need to take her time going down. When her legs got tired, she pulled out her dive computer and watched it as she slowly descended to the bottom.

She sat there and looked up at the surface. Just for a minute.

High above her head, the top of the ocean wavered and sparkled like an alien sky.

She could do this a thousand times and it would never get old. Never. She was *breathing* underwater. Sitting in the middle of this huge aquatic world that most people never got to see.

At first glance, there wasn't much to see here. The visibility wasn't great. But as she slowly kicked her fins and explored along the bottom, sea creatures began to appear from the murky depths. There were spiny red fish drifting over the rocks and spiky sea urchins clinging tight. She pointed her camera in their direction, unsure of whether it was capturing anything or not. The screen had a habit of going black while it was still recording, and there was nothing she could do about it with these gloves on.

A huge lobster eyed her distrustfully, sitting still as a stone.

She saw bright dots of white and pulled herself along the rocks to examine a strange creature covered in soft, undulating spikes. At first, she thought that it might be a tiny sea anemone, but it wasn't the right shape.

It was a sea slug, she realized. Each of the crimson spikes

along its body had a bright white tip, like the fingers of a tiny gremlin. She stared, immobile, until the cold began to seep into her bones. Then, she pushed away from the rocks and kicked her fins.

A school of fish flitted over the rocks a few yards away, and she swam towards them.

She hated to admit it, but Gabe wasn't kidding. The water was *cold*. She could feel it penetrating her limbs like ice. She began to realize that she might have overestimated the length of time she'd booked Gabe's boat each day.

Maybe she should have invested in a dry suit. The thousand-dollar price tag had scared her away, but she was beginning to regret that decision.

But hey, this was just her first day. She would adapt to the cold. It's not like she was diving under the polar ice.

This was *at least* eight degrees warmer.

Fallyn turned to work her way back towards the boat when a strange shape caught her eye. Something massive and wooden and half buried in the sand.

No way.

Not on her first day.

What were the chances?

But it was, Fallyn realized as she moved closer.

It was a wooden chest.

A *treasure* chest?

Her whole body trembled as she swam towards it.

She brushed away a layer of sand and tried to jimmy the lock open. As she worked, Fallyn realized that it wasn't old enough to be a long-lost pirate treasure chest. It looked more modern, like something her mother would use to store blankets.

Her heart sank, but only slightly. It might not be the chest that she was looking for, but she had found half-buried treasure her first day out. It felt like a promising start to her adventure.

She checked her dive computer. Plenty of air left. Her face was numb, but whatever. She was on an adventure! A real adventure. Heart hammering, she picked up a rock from the sandy ocean floor and beat on the lid around the lock until a chunk of the waterlogged wood broke away.

For a second, she stared at the chest, a strange dread dampening her excitement. Then, she took a deep breath and pushed the lid open.

Almost immediately, a ghostly, blue-gray object drifted up, level with her face.

A human hand.

Fallyn pushed herself away from the chest, then coughed and sputtered as icy water filled her mouth. In her shock, the scuba regulator had fallen from her mouth. She groped for the tube that attached it to the air tank, then followed the line down to the bottom and pulled the regulator to her face.

Fallyn took several deep breaths. Then, she swam forward and, pushing back a wave of terror, peered down into the chest.

She hadn't found buried treasure.

She'd found a dead body.

2

CEE-CEE

"Who's Nana's little girl?" Cee-cee crooned. "Gracie is!"

Her heart was so filled with love, it felt like it might burst.

Gabe and Sasha's baby was beyond perfect. A tiny angel with luminous gray eyes and tufts of soft, dark hair. She was wide awake this morning, staring right into her grandmother's eyes. That feeling took Cee-cee back to her own infants, those early days with Gabe and Max. She hadn't been sure if it would be possible without the massive hit of endorphins that came with birth and breastfeeding, but she loved this baby girl just as much as she had loved her own newborn babies. If anything, the fact that she slept peacefully each night just funneled more energy into her love for this perfect little grand-baby.

Cee-cee was so in love with being a Nana that she could hardly stand herself. She smiled as she remembered the trio of acquaintances she had cornered at her cupcake shop that morning. She'd just pulled a chair up to their table and shown them a dozen photos of Gracie on her phone. Already she was one of those grandparents who would show pictures to strangers in line at the grocery store — and she knew that she would only get worse as Gracie grew and began vaulting over one milestone after another. Rolling over, crawling, talking...

There was so much to look forward to. So what if people thought her a fool? She was all in and happy about it. As a matter of fact, Cee-cee had never been so happy in all her life.

She almost felt guilty about that — after all, she had loved her own babies more than life itself and always would.

And yet, the stress and exhaustion that came with motherhood was like nothing she could have imagined. Going months without deep, restorative sleep. Bickering with her husband. Then, the trials of parenting a newborn and a toddler at the same time.

Becoming a grandmother was different. Pure, weightless joy, unadulterated by fears of inadequacy and sleepless nights—not to mention a strained and stressful marriage. She got to experience all the best parts of parenting.

She cast a compassionate look at Sasha, who looked as exhausted as any new mother.

"Did you get any sleep last night?"

"Not really." Sasha gave her a tired smile. "She wakes up every time I put her down."

"Max was like that," Cee-cee told her. "Gabe was easy. He would fall asleep by himself in his crib, even when he was tiny. I could just feed him and put him down and walk away. But Max had to be held all the time — and I had Gabe running riot at that point, mind you. He wasn't so easy once he learned to run. Max would never sleep in her crib. Not once. Even if she was asleep already, she would wake up the moment I set her down."

"What did you do?"

"I slept with her. Nate wouldn't hear of having her in bed, and his mother insisted that I was spoiling her, that I should just let her cry herself to sleep and she would learn. I tried it once or twice — Nate was so insistent — but it was the worst kind of torture. It just ripped my heart out to hear her scream like that. So I ended up moving the mattress from our guest bedroom into the nursery, and I slept in the same bed with her every night for over four years. At least, until she fell asleep... once she was two or three, I could usually sneak away. Though there were nights that she would come crawling into my bed in tears, asking why I had left her all alone. Even at five, she would only fall asleep without me once we put her in the same room as Gabe."

Gracie began to root and fuss, and Cee-cee handed her back to Sasha.

"I think she's hungry. You feed her, and then I'll feed you. I think that soup is nearly done."

"Bless you, Cee-cee," Sasha whispered. There were tears in her eyes and hesitation in her voice as she corrected herself, calling her mother-in-law by the name that Cee-cee had invited her to use months before. "*Mom.* You've done so much for us that there's nothing I have to do but keep Gracie fed and clean."

"That's all you should have to do," Cee-cee said firmly. "Most cultures give mothers a solid month — forty days, even — to focus on nothing but caring for their babies and getting strong again. Heck, some countries give women a year off work. My mother took care of me, and I'll take care of you. That's what family does."

"I don't know what we would have done without you."

"You would have coped," Cee-cee said simply. "But I'm happy to help. Besides, it gives me an excuse to see Gracie all the time. You just sit back. Come into the kitchen whenever you're ready to eat. I'll just go check on that soup."

Sasha smiled at her and leaned back into her throne of pillows, loosening her robe to feed baby Gracie. Cee-cee walked through the small house and into the kitchen, where she peeked at the chicken soup that simmered on the stove. Done — and it smelled amazing. She turned off the burner and dove into the dishes.

There was a knock on the front door, and Cee-cee called, "Come in!"

Anna walked in carrying two large bags. She kicked off her boots, tossed one bag onto the couch, and came into the kitchen.

"You're just in time for chicken soup," Cee-cee said.

"Oh no," Anna laughed. "I brought chicken soup too! Piping hot, too."

"You did not!"

"Coconut chicken soup from that amazing new Thai place."

"Oh, good! Completely different flavor profile. Grandma's chicken soup is better the next day anyway. I'll just put it in the freezer before I leave. What's in the other bag?"

"Clothes," Anna said. "Mostly six months and up, so bigger than the stuff that people gave her at the baby shower. Eva gave them to me for Sasha when I went into the diner for breakfast. They belonged to... her niece's neighbor, or something like that? I don't know. You know Eva, I can hardly keep up with her or process what she said before she's racing off to the next table."

Cee-cee smiled fondly and shook her head. "The energy that woman has, and at her age..."

"You're not doing so bad yourself, Grandma."

"Ha ha." An idea occurred to her as she rinsed the last of the dishes. "What do you think of using those same Thai flavors in a cupcake?"

Anna eyed her dubiously.

"Not with chicken or the really savory elements." Cee-cee rolled her eyes. "Just with those Thai lime leaves, galangal, lemongrass, ginger... Coconut-lime cupcakes with lemongrass icing and candied ginger. Something like that."

"Okay, that does sound pretty good." Anna pulled three bowls down from the cupboard.

"Probably not any time soon, though. I have my hands full as it is, and I want to be here for Sasha."

"World's best grandma."

"It's not exactly selfless. I'm addicted to that new baby smell. Speaking of which," she said as Sasha walked in. "Let me hold her while you eat."

"She's sleeping," Sasha said uncertainly. "What if she wakes up?"

"That's alright. Come on, you need sustenance."

"And a shower," she said with a wry smile.

"You can have both. In whichever order you like. Come here, Gracie, my sweet." Cee-cee slipped her arms under Sasha's and gently took her granddaughter. Gracie stirred but didn't wake.

"When do I get a turn?" asked Anna in a stage whisper.

"You two eat," Cee-cee said. "Then you can hold her while I have some soup and Sasha takes a shower. Or a nice long bath," she suggested with a smile.

Anna served up two bowls of Tom Kha Gai and Sasha joined her at the table.

"How's Teddy?" Sasha asked. Before Anna could answer, Sasha took a small sip of soup and exclaimed, "Wow! That is delicious!"

"Good, right?" Anna's face lit up as she said, "Teddy's great. His parents are still pulling crazy hours, so he's with us three nights a week. I swear he learns twenty new words a day and has such a curious mind. It's amazing."

Cee-cee smiled as her sister continued to chatter about Beckett's grandson. She had never seen her baby sister so happy. Excited about her next adventure, sure. Or laughing over recent ones. But this was different. There was a love and fulfillment that turned her excitement into true joy.

The woman who had always been terrified of growing roots — of getting stuck in one place and not able to live her dreams — was now mired in a tangle of roots and loving it. She had a true partner in Beckett and loved her role as grandma to his grandson Teddy.

She even had a whole new family in Cherry Blossom Point: a father who adored her and three sisters who were coming to love her nearly as much as Cee-cee did. Even her cranky older brother, Jack, was coming around a bit.

At a lull in the conversation, she asked, "How is everyone in Cherry Blossom Point? Have you heard from them lately?"

"A bit," Anna replied. "They've all been busy with work, but they're doing well. And I've been seeing Eric every week for flying lessons." As usual, she looked a tad guilty when she mentioned her biological father's name.

"You know," Cee-cee said gently, "building a relationship with him will never take away from the bond you had with Pop."

"I know," Anna said. Some of the tension went out of her face. "It's been... kind of wonderful, honestly. Getting to know him. Surreal, but good. I'm getting better about not beating myself up about it, too."

"And how about Gayle? How is she coping?" The eldest Merrill sister had been struggling recently after leaving a long, unhappy marriage, and Cee-cee knew all too well what that was like.

But Anna just smiled and said, "She's past it. The divorce is final. She had to give up The Milky Thistle as part of the settlement, but she's starting a new bar with her best friend. More of a rustic, woodsy theme this time. It sounds fantastic."

"Good for her! Keep me posted, and we can all drive down together when it opens. Make a weekend of it, maybe."

"Is this just an excuse to have a girl's weekend and drink too much wine?" Anna asked, laughing.

Cee-cee stuck her tongue out at her sister — there was something about siblings that kept a person's inner child alive — and looked back down at Gracie's perfect face. She could hardly keep her eyes off of her.

She liked Gayle. Understood her. Even though her younger siblings thought she was too controlling, Cee-cee knew that it came from a place of love. Love and fear, maybe... it could be hard to disentangle the two, sometimes. Cee-cee knew what it was like to be the oldest, to feel responsible for her siblings. And that was with a tiny age gap.

Gayle was nearly grown when Nikki was still small; it was no wonder if she felt an even heavier burden of responsibility than Cee-cee did.

She was glad that Gayle had grown and softened some, allowing Anna into her life despite her initial misgivings. Cee-cee respected that. It was no easy thing, starting over as a middle-aged woman on so many levels. But she had done it, and she was happier than she'd ever been. She wished the same thing for Gayle.

"Earth to Cee-cee!" Anna called from across the kitchen. Cee-cee looked up with a start.

"I *said*, how are things at the cupcake shop." Anna refilled one of the soup bowls and set it in front of Sasha, who thanked her with a shy smile.

"It's been packed the past few weeks," she said happily. "Business is so good that I've been thinking of converting my apartment above the shop into an extra seating area... it has such a beautiful view of the ocean. But I'm so reluctant to give it up! Where else can I watch the sun rise over the water from my bed? I'm spoiled."

"There are ways you could expand without giving up your home," Sasha said. "I'd be happy to help. Perks of having an interior designer for a daughter-in-law. It would be the perfect thing to keep my brain from turning to mush while I'm home with Gracie."

"Mick suggested the same thing recently, but I'm loath to turn the place into a construction zone just before tourist season. You know that kind of thing is never finished in time. Maybe next year. Besides," she added with a conspiratorial grin, "we have a wedding to plan for."

Anna spun around in her seat, and Sasha gasped. "Wait, what? You're finally going to do it?"

Cee-cee laughed. "Yep. No more putting it off. First Pop passed away, and then Max was so stressed out over her father's debts. And of course we didn't want to plan it too close to Gracie being born. But now that she's here and you're both healthy, and Ian's loan bailed Nate out of dire straits... I feel like I can finally focus on *us*."

"An early summer wedding!" Anna exclaimed. "Outdoors, I hope?"

"Too chancy, no?" Sasha asked. "A big old church with high ceilings, maybe? But don't we need more time to plan?"

"I want to take advantage of this window of opportunity while it's still open," Cee-cee replied. "A family this size, you never know when the next crisis will be. Knock on wood. Anyway, I'm not twenty anymore. I don't need a big fancy party. I just need Mick and all of the people I love most there to celebrate with us."

"We'll be there," Anna said, "wherever it is, come hell or high water. You could get married on top of Mt. Everest and I wouldn't miss it."

"If you haven't climbed that mountain yet it's only because there are no interesting animals at the top for you to photograph," said Cee-cee with a laugh.

Sasha slurped up the rest of her soup and stood to reclaim her daughter.

"Come on. Have some of the coconut chicken soup, Nana," she said. "It's delicious."

Cee-cee planted a light kiss on her granddaughter's forehead before handing her back to Sasha.

The truth was, she didn't much care *where* she and Mick got married. So long as her family was there.

She smiled as she fixed herself a bowl of soup, thinking how blessed she was to have such a loving family to share in her joy — and how very grateful she was.

3

FALLYN

It took two hours on land and a scalding hot bath for Fallyn to get her core temperature up.

Recovering from the dive emotionally? That was going to take more time.

A lot more time.

As long as she lived, Fallyn would never forget the image of that skeletal hand floating up in front of her face. It was seared into her psyche. It would be the story she told on repeat at the old folks home, like her grandmother who never spoke the last two years of her life except to announce with inordinate pride that her poodle had taken Best of Breed *and* Best of Variety at a statewide competition in 1963.

Fallyn had seen more horrific things than the long-dead corpse she'd found that afternoon.

More horrors than she could count. More than any human brain should have to process.

And yet, the storybook horror of that gray-blue hand had imprinted itself in the deepest layers of her brain. She could feel it.

"Are you here for dinner, honey? Or just a slice of pie?"

Fallyn blinked up at the sweet-faced, elderly waitress who stood just a couple feet away. She hadn't noticed her walk up to the table.

"Both," she said woodenly. "Please."

"Take a look at this menu and I'll be back in a tick. Shout me down if you'd like. My name's Eva."

"Thank you, Eva." Fallyn tried to smile, but it felt more like a grimace.

"Anything to drink? Coffee?"

Fallyn was tempted, but she knew from experience that coffee on top of frayed nerves was a terrible idea. "Chamomile tea?" she asked hopefully.

Eva patted her on the shoulder. "Coming right up, hon."

Her stomach was a ravenous pit after exercising in the frigid Maine water, but she was having trouble focusing on the menu. Her brain clicked restlessly from one channel to another.

The look on Gabe's face when she'd told him what she'd found.

Detective Ethan Jenkins over the phone, calm and gracious as he thanked her for calling in her find.

The curled form of a body that had spent years — probably decades — in a small wooden trunk.

Three small, bloody corpses on a cold concrete floor.

She hadn't stuck around to talk to the cops, though she had agreed to follow up with Detective Jenkins later this week. She had been shaking with cold and shock, even after she changed into dry clothes. She'd left her car in the harbor parking lot and taken an Uber back to the inn where she was staying.

Fallyn put her menu down on the table. Her hands came down hard enough to make a noise that startled her. When Eva returned with her tea, Fallyn gave her a pleading look.

"What do you recommend?" she asked, wrapping her hands around the warm mug.

"How about some classic comfort food, hon? Burger and fries?"

Fallyn gave her a shaky smile. "Perfect. Thank you. Cheddar?"

"You've got it." The woman gave her another motherly pat on the shoulder before walking away.

Fallyn pulled out her laptop and tried to distract herself with research for her treasure hunt, but the whole thing felt tainted now. Worse than that, it felt foolish. Unimportant.

Without even making a conscious decision, she opened up the video she had downloaded a couple of hours before. She had already sent it to Detective Jenkins. No doubt she could sell it, if she were so inclined. She wasn't.

Fallyn clicked through the short video frame by frame, examining the cadaver for some clue she might have missed, some indicator of how long it had been down there.

A glint of gold caught her eye, and she leaned in for a better look.

Then, Eva appeared by her shoulder, and Fallyn jumped. She snapped the laptop shut, feeling like a child who had been caught looking at something they shouldn't.

"Here's your dinner, hon." She set down a plate that was piled high with golden fries. The hamburger was thick, and topped with cheese that looked like it was made of actual milk rather than plastic. Fallyn was grateful she'd taken a chance on this place; she was never sure of what she'd get at a diner.

"That was quick. Thank you. It smells amazing."

"We aim to please," Eva said amiably.

Fallyn's stomach growled, and she resisted tearing into the cheeseburger like a half-starved dog. Eva was still looking at her. Fallyn dipped a hot fry in ketchup and bit into it. Perfectly crispy on the outside, soft and fluffy on the inside.

"Is this your first time in Bluebird Bay?" Eva asked.

"It is. I'm staying at the Seal Pup Inn."

"Oh, Molly's place! I stayed there once, when an old boyfriend kicked me out. This was a terribly long time ago, mind. She'd only just taken over running the place. But she wouldn't take a dime from me. Insisted on putting me up until I was back on my feet. Of course, it wasn't tourist season. But still, she's a good egg. It's a beautiful building, isn't it?"

"It's lovely." Fallyn had chosen it for that reason. The handsome wooden house was a stark contrast to the series of apartments she had lived in for the past twenty years, little boxes in monoliths of glass and steel.

"Her grandfather built it," Eva said. "Well, had it built, I suppose would be more accurate. Over a century ago, now. They just don't make them like that anymore."

Fallyn ate another fry, unsure of what to say, and Eva gave her a knowing smile.

"I'll leave you to enjoy your dinner, hon."

Fallyn devoured her food in three minutes flat.

Eva came back straightaway, looking impressed. "Can I get you a warm slice of pie? We have apple or blueberry. Or a cool slice of lemon meringue."

"One of each," Fallyn said impulsively. "Please." She couldn't remember the last time she was so hungry.

Eva grinned. "I like you."

She returned in short order with Fallyn's herculean dessert. Fallyn picked up a fork and worked through the decadent plate of food slowly, savoring the warm fruit and the cool tang of the lemon meringue.

She opened her laptop, angling it away from the rest of the diner, and looked at her video again.

What did it say about her that she could do this while eating apple pie?

That she'd stayed at her Chicago job for far too long, that's what.

Fallyn heaved a sigh and zoomed in on the glint of gold that had caught her eye earlier. An earring. No, make that two earrings. A double piercing in one ear... or what remained of it. The chest and frigid water had preserved the corpse to a gruesome degree. It had basically been sitting in a fridge.

There was a small gold hoop and something else... she zoomed in further, and realized that it was shaped like a heart. It was a bit of plastic that was probably pink at some point, or maybe red. At this depth, everything was tinged blue.

How long had plastic earrings been around? In the shape of a heart, no less. Almost certainly after the seventies. And a double piercing... safe to say that the body hadn't been lying there for a century.

A quick internet search showed only five disappearances in this part of Maine within the past fifty years. She disregarded the three men, which left her with two teenage girls.

Runaways.

At least, that's what they were called.

Robin Sanders and Emily Addison.

Robin was found months later in another town, shacked up with her drug dealer.

But Emily was never found.

Fallyn looked through the few pictures of the girl that she could find. Long brown hair, big brown eyes. She was seventeen when she disappeared, though she looked younger in these photos. She wore bright colors... and had two piercings in each ear.

Fallyn closed the computer and took another bite of her lemon meringue pie.

If Detective Jenkins didn't make the connection himself, she would fill him in.

But that's it. That's where her involvement ended.

Fallyn paid her bill, leaving a hefty tip for the kind old waitress, and walked back the half mile to her inn. There were streetlights to guide her way, but nearly all of the shops and cafes were closed. Small town life. So different from Chicago.

Of course, heinous things still happened in small towns.

Even when she stopped chasing them, they still seemed to find her.

Why *was* that? What sort of karma was she working off? Was she on her fourth incarnation, post Jack the Ripper, or what?

But she had a choice. She could simply choose to step away.

A quick chat with that detective tomorrow, and she could let it go. She didn't have to read the news stories that were sure to surface. She could just do what she came here to do and then leave. She could even leave now and come back to search for treasure in the summertime when the weather was less frigid and she had recovered from the shock of finding... well, something she hadn't been looking for. Something she had been trying to distance herself from.

When Fallyn walked into the inn, Molly was there at the front desk. The sixty-something-year-old owner lived at the inn, somewhere towards the back of the first floor. She had a comfortable-looking chair behind the desk where she liked to lounge with her e-reader, popping up like a Jack-in-the-box every time someone walked in.

Molly's smile was so bright in contrast to Fallyn's dour mood that she found herself squinting.

"Welcome home! How was dinner?"

"It was delicious," Fallyn said honestly. "I'm stuffed. And tired."

"I was just about to turn in myself," Molly said brightly, "but I sleep better knowing that everyone is safe in their beds. Is there anything I can get you?"

"I'm fine, thank you."

"Sweet dreams, then. You're welcome to stay in for breakfast tomorrow. My daughter's coming by first thing, and we're going to make crumpets. I have the most fabulous assortment of jams and jellies, and I make real old-fashioned clotted cream. Gina's crumpets are out of this world. You'll love them. You're welcome to join us in the kitchen, or just give me a ring and I'll bring you breakfast in bed."

Fallyn stood stiff under this onslaught of maternal

energy. Women like this always made her wonder what it would have been like to have a mother like that. Growing up, she had watched her friends' mothers with bewilderment and barely-contained jealousy when they petted and praised their daughters.

Her own mother was reserved and, well, not particularly maternal. She had done her best — Fallyn had fond memories of her mother reading Lord of the Rings out loud, or taking her for long walks through the woods — but beyond being pulled by her hand through a crowd, she had no memories of her mother ever actually touching her. She supposed that must be an exaggeration, but it was how she remembered her childhood. So when other mothers were so filled with love and affection that it spilled over onto strangers, Fallyn was never sure how to respond.

Molly's smile dimmed a bit. "Are you alright, Fallyn?"

Fallyn nodded and offered her a shaky smile. "I'm fine. Thank you. Just exhausted."

She had her foot on the first step of the staircase when a question tore through her mind. She tried to force herself upstairs, but her curiosity had always been a wild, feral thing. It had a mind of its own.

"Molly?" Fallyn turned to face the older woman. "Do you know who Emily Addison is?"

"Goodness." Molly's eyebrows shot up, but her expression stayed pleasant. "I haven't heard that name in a very long time."

Fallyn swallowed. It was awkward asking questions without using her journalistic persona to shield her, but she pushed forward. "I was looking through old news stories about Bluebird Bay... I saw that she went missing in the mid-nineties. Was she ever found?"

Molly shook her head slowly. "She went to school with my daughter, Gina. Emily was a grade or two below her, so they didn't know each other well. But it was a shock to the whole school, when she disappeared. To the whole town, really. Things like that just don't happen in Bluebird Bay. The police eventually gave up, said she was a runaway. After her eighteenth birthday, they just threw up their hands and stopped looking. But her mother always insisted that Emily wouldn't just run away..." Molly shook her head slowly. "Her poor mother. She never believed her girl was gone for good."

"I'm sorry to hear that," Fallyn said softly. "Thanks for filling me in."

Molly brightened. "I have some pictures of her, if you'd like?"

"Oh, no, you don't have to go through all that."

"It's no trouble at all. Just wait there for one minute, would you? I'll be right back. Don't go away."

Molly rushed off down the hallway and returned a minute later with a stack of thick books.

"All of Gina's high school yearbooks. She was ready to throw them away, if you can believe that. I wouldn't hear of it, so I kept them safe. They live on my shelf with all of our family albums."

Fallyn forced a smile and took the heavy books. She didn't want to offend the kind innkeeper.

"Thank you, Molly."

"No trouble at all, dear. Just leave them on my desk when you're through with them, and I'll see them home."

Fallyn carried the yearbooks upstairs to her room and

began to flip through them. She chose the one from 1995, Gina's senior year. Emily's junior year.

Her final year.

Emily Addison was on the first page of her class photos, smiling awkwardly at the school photographer. Fallyn flipped through the other pages, searching for Emily. She didn't seem to be in many clubs, no sports teams... but there she was, smiling from the bleachers at a football game. There was another photo of her walking down the hall with a textbook clutched to her chest.

In the first picture, Emily was beaming. She looked young and happy, full of school spirit.

In the second, her eyes were downcast and her shoulders hunched forward. She had traded her bright, revealing clothes for an oversized sweatshirt, and grief hung around her like a miasma.

Fallyn closed the book with a sigh.

Who hurt you, Emily Addison?

4

ANNA

IF SEVENTEEN-YEAR-OLD ANNA could see herself now, she'd never believe it. In her senior year of high school, she had been ready to fly the coop for good. It had always seemed to Anna that her mother and the other women in Bluebird Bay lived a sort of half-life, always setting aside their wants and needs to tend to their husbands and children. That would *not* be her.

She was going to skip town on her eighteenth birthday and never look back.

Of course, she had never actually gone a year without coming home to Bluebird Bay. This was her home, and her family was here. The longer she stayed away, the more she missed it. Appreciated it.

Still, she never thought that she would settle down. Sure, she kept an apartment in town — but that was just for the sake of convenience, to have a place of her own to rest up between trips and edit her photos instead of always crashing with family. Over the years, though, her stays at home had gotten longer and her work trips jet-setting around the world became less frequent. The thought of hitting fifty countries in a single year like she'd done at twenty-seven was exhausting instead of exhilarating, as it had been then. She still felt a fierce pride and love for the person she had been then... but she didn't actually want to *be* that person anymore. Not entirely.

She still felt that wanderlust now and again. But now it was more about revisiting the magical places she had discovered over the years, reconnecting with old friends, and sharing those things with Beckett.

She flashed him a grin over her shoulder, and he smiled back. Beckett was sitting at the breakfast table with a newspaper while she made coffee and toast.

Beckett cooked for them most nights, and so she was happy to throw together a rough facsimile of breakfast each morning; he never complained when it was toast ten days in a row. This domestic chapter of her life felt so wholesome, and Anna was still amazed at what profound *joy* she found in such a simple daily routine.

It had taken fifty years, but Anna had finally met a man worth sticking around for. Beckett had welcomed her into his beautiful craftsman-style home and into his family; she loved his grandson Teddy as if he were her own flesh and blood, and the small boy spent enough time with them that Anna felt like she was getting a taste of that motherhood journey she had never made time for. She loved her nieces and nephews dearly, but she had missed most of their early milestones during those wild years of building her career. With Teddy, she was there for all of it. And she was all in.

Still, she wouldn't be Anna Sullivan without travel and photography. She took pictures for a local wildlife rescue and had dragged Beckett to Hawaii not once but twice, where she had photographed monk seals and manta rays. More recently, she had finally convinced him to get a passport — his first. They were still deliberating where they would go on their first international adventure. There were so many places to choose from, and Anna wasn't in a terrible rush. Her trip to Cherry Blossom Point had given her plenty of excitement to tide her over for a while, and she was profoundly grateful to be home again.

Anna checked her phone and found a message from Eric: a rather blurry photo of a rose-breasted grosbeak with the words *Wish you were here! My photos never do them justice.*

She smiled and replied, *Let's go bird watching together soon. Before next week's flying lesson, maybe?*

Eric replied immediately. *It's a date!*

Love and gratitude and grief swirled through Anna's chest. Her feelings about her birth father were still complicated, but she was deeply grateful for the chance to get to know Eric Merrill and his four children — her half siblings. Nikki Merrill had given her a precious gift when she came barreling into their lives the year before. And she had kept holding it out in offering, even after Anna threw it back in her face a time or two.

When Anna invited herself to go to Cherry Blossom Point with Nikki a few months before, she'd hoped for a chance to reconnect with her birth father and get some sort of closure. Flash forward to now, and she'd gotten a whole second family out of the deal.

It was amazing how far they had come in such a short time. Things were still strained between Anna and her brother, Jack, but her relationships with the rest of the

Merrill clan were nearly as dear to her as her relationships with Cee-cee and Steph, the sisters she had known all her life.

"They just announced the news," Beckett said quietly, looking up from his newspaper. "The body belonged to Emily after all."

His words were like a sudden rain cloud drifting in front of the mellow morning sunshine of her thoughts, and Anna's stomach sank. She set their food and coffee down on the table, but she wasn't feeling particularly hungry.

When Cee-cee had called her and Steph earlier that week with the news, they had all been left reeling. They didn't know yet whose body it was, only that the tourist that Cee-cee's son Gabe had taken out on his boat had found human remains in a trunk at the bottom of the ocean. Surely they couldn't belong to Steph's deceased husband, Paul?

Logically, they'd known how unlikely it was, but hope was a strange thing...

Anna hadn't even been sure of what to hope for. It seemed bizarre and gruesome to *wish* for the police to discover her brother-in-law's body on the sea floor... but she knew how much it hurt Stephanie and her children that Paul had never been laid to rest. Finding his body at long last would have given them some belated closure.

But their hopes had been dashed when Ethan had called shortly after, stating that they had already determined that the remains belonged to a female. Once they'd gotten over their initial disappointment, the sisters had put it aside... except for Cee-cee, who recalled a girl going missing when they were in their twenties. Emily Addison was her name. But all three were quick to realize it could've been a woman from any town, even hundreds of miles away, who had just been dropped off the coast of Bluebird Bay or moved there by ocean currents over the years.

Anna had to admit, she was surprised to find out now that Cee-cee's guess had been right.

She circled around the table to look over Beckett's shoulder at the news story. Emily's picture beamed bright and happy, blissfully ignorant of the future that awaited her. She was only seventeen. The photo was familiar, and Anna instantly recalled where she had seen it.

Everywhere.

All around town, at least a hundred times over.

"That's the picture that her mother used," she said sadly. "I remember Patty Addison posting missing notices all over town for months. Years, maybe. Long after the police had ruled Emily a runaway." Anna heaved a sigh and leaned into Beckett, wrapping her arms around his shoulders. "That poor woman."

She couldn't imagine how terrible that must be, having someone you loved disappear. Being left to wonder where they were, if they were safe, if they were hurt or scared... Her mind flicked back to the fire that had destroyed her childhood home just a couple years ago. They hadn't known whether or not their father was inside, and the terror of not knowing had been absolute torture. They had found him, safe and unharmed, that same day.

But to lose your *child* and go your whole life without knowing?

It was enough to drive a person mad.

Anna pressed her cheek against Beckett's, feeling grateful all over again for their snug, secure, predictable life. She would enjoy it while she could; Lord knew there were no guarantees.

Anna's phone rang and she went to answer it. Her eldest sister's photo lit up the screen.

"Hi Cee-cee," Anna said as she raised the phone to her ear.

Her sister chuckled. "Remember the days of house phones? When you just had to pick up and it was a mystery who would be on the other line?"

"Did you see the news?" Anna cut in.

"No. What happened?" The worry in Cee-cee's voice was evident.

"It *was* her. Emily. That girl who disappeared back in the nineties."

"Oh, God. Her poor mother," Cee-cee murmured.

"I never pictured something like this happening in Bluebird Bay. I mean, sure, there was that guy who got mauled to death by that bear a few years back. And Paul... but back when *this* happened, I still thought that Bluebird Bay was the kind of town where nothing *ever* happened, you know? I remember thinking that the police must be right, that she was just a runaway teenager. I could certainly understand the impulse," Anna added wryly. She shook her head and pulled her attention back to the present. "Anyway, sorry to be the grim reaper. You sounded like you were in a great mood when you called. What's up?"

"It's okay, kiddo. That's big news." Cee-cee was quiet for a moment. Then, she said, "I was calling to see if you're up for a cupcake brunch tomorrow."

"Always," Anna shot back. "Yes."

"I'm thinking ten? The shop's usually calm then, and

Stephanie has a couple of hours between classes. I was hoping we could have a little brainstorm session, come up with some wedding ideas and plans. I want to keep it small and simple, I know that, but I'm not sure what exactly I want to do. Or where I want to have the ceremony."

"Count me in." It would be good to have something happy and hopeful to focus her attention on.

"Thanks! Hey, three more people just walked into the shop. The line's getting long. I'm gonna go help out. See you tomorrow."

Anna disconnected, and Beckett looked up.

"What's the plan?" he asked.

"That was Cee-cee. I'm going to head over to her cupcake shop tomorrow morning to start figuring out her wedding plans. She has a phenomenal photographer on hand, *obviously*, but other than that she needs some help figuring things out." She paused and looked at him, cocking her head to one side.

"What's that look for?" he asked, wary of being pulled into her scheming.

"It just occurred to me that you never really knew the old Cee-cee. You just know the new-and-improved, post-Nate Cee-cee."

Beckett smiled at her. "Is she really that different?"

"In some ways," Anna said thoughtfully. She sat down and began dressing her toast with a generous helping of elderberry jam. "She's always been maternal, and super empathetic. Even when we were little girls. But when she was married to Nate, she was always so prim and proper. Never really relaxed. She hardly ever even ate the stuff that she baked, because her asinine husband was always making remarks about her gaining weight. Cee-cee lived in Nate's shadow. She was always so unsure of herself."

"You're right," Beckett said with a frown. "Knowing her now, that's hard to imagine."

"I'm so happy for her. That she found herself and her passion. Marrying a man who appreciates all those parts of her is just the icing on the cupcake. I feel like this celebration is about more than Cee-cee and Mick getting together. I want to celebrate everything she's accomplished and all of the growing she's done these past few years."

"I'm happy for her too. For both of them. They're good together." Beckett squeezed Anna's hand and then released it, and they fell into their usual peaceful morning silence as they sipped their coffee and read the paper.

When Anna turned the page and saw that smiling picture of Emily Addison, though, she dropped her toast and wiped her sticky fingertips on a napkin.

Suddenly, she didn't feel like eating anymore.

That girl could've been Nikki's daughter, Beth, or a younger Max. Just a normal kid, bright and hopeful. But she never had the chance to grow into herself. To find her passion. To find love. To marry, if she chose. Her life was cut short so young, and so cruelly. It was utterly senseless and heartbreaking.

Anna thought again of Mrs. Addison, putting up new posters again and again, season after season, and she shuddered. Was Emily's mother still alive? If so, Anna hoped that this would give her some closure... but she thought that it was more likely to reopen an old wound.

Instead of simply living with the grief of loss, wondering where Emily had gone, hoping that her daughter had built a beautiful life for herself somewhere... now Patty Addison had to grapple with a whole new set of fears.

Did she suffer?

Who did this to her?

And the one that was currently gripping Anna herself...

What if that person was still out there somewhere, in another small town, hunting more girls like Emily?

5

MARYANNE

When Maryanne Carpenter Brown saw Emily's picture in the newspaper, that same picture that Patty Addison had plastered all over town year after year, she went into autopilot. Just snatched up her car keys and walked out the door without pausing to think. She still knew the way to the Addison house by heart, even though she hadn't been there in over twenty years.

Then, she realized that she was driving to Patty's house uninvited *and* empty-handed. So she'd turned her car around and gone home to make some comfort food before setting out again. Her grandmother's meatball recipe took most of the morning, and it was midday by the time she got back in her car.

Maryanne knew Emily well. Or she had, when she was fourteen and Emily was nine. She used to babysit for Patty every weekend; the single mother worked ten-hour days on Saturdays in order to make up for leaving work at three o'clock every weekday to be with her kids after school. It had been the perfect job, getting paid to watch cartoons and play board games with the little sister she'd always wanted. Emily was smart and shy, with long brown hair and big brown eyes.

A memory flashed through Maryanne's head, clear as the road in front of her. Emily rushing to greet her mother when she got home from work, crowning her with the daisy chain that she and Maryanne had made together at the park that day. Patty had looked dead tired when she'd walked in, but the moment she saw her daughter, she shone with such joy and love that her whole face lit up.

And then, when she was just seventeen, Emily had disappeared.

In the months after Emily's disappearance, Maryanne did what she could to support Patty. Emily's mother had no husband, no extended family that Maryanne knew of, and her son was on active duty overseas. On the days that she saw Patty going around town tearing down the missing person signs that were too weathered to read and posting new ones, Maryanne would always drop off a casserole for dinner. Patty had done that month after month after month, long after the police had given up on Emily. They had told Patty that her daughter was a runaway, even though she had insisted time and again that Emily would never run away from home like that.

At first, Maryanne would bring her dinner with words of hope, assuring her that the police would find Emily soon. After a while, she had tried to offer her condolences instead... but Patty didn't want to hear it. She shut everyone out and stopped answering her phone. Sometimes, when Maryanne showed up at her door with dinner, Patty would greet her with an unnerving brightness and talk about what life would be like when Emily came home, how much schoolwork she would have to catch up on, how she would have to repeat her senior year, how much she hoped that Emily's big brother, Joseph, would leave the army and come back to Maine so that they could all be a family again.

And then her son died overseas.

After that, she accepted Maryanne's condolences in grim silence.

Maryanne hadn't known Joseph very well, but Emily had worshiped her big brother. The few times that Maryanne had seen him, he had doted on his baby sister. They had been such a happy family. No father to speak of, but Patty was more loving than both of Maryanne's parents put together. She worked hard all week and showered Emily with attention when she was home.

Patty went on putting up the missing posters, year after year. After Joseph died, she seemed to be doing it more out of habit than out of any real hope that she might see one of her children again. She only left her house to tear down the worn and faded posters, post new ones, and buy a month's worth of canned food. She kept trying long after the rest of the world had more or less forgotten that Emily had ever existed.

And Emily had never been found. She had never come home. Not alive. Not even in a box.

She had just disappeared off the face of the Earth.

Into the Gulf of Maine, apparently.

The cold, dark depths of the sea.

What an utterly heartrending ending for such a sweet, bright girl.

Maryanne realized that she had been sitting in her car for a good while, just idling in front of Patty's house. She shut off the engine and lifted the crockpot of meatballs from the floor of the passenger's side. With a basket of rolls balanced precariously on top of the crockpot, she strode up the path to Patty's front door and hit the doorbell with her elbow.

Would Patty even remember her?

Should she even be here? She had no way of knowing if Patty even lived here anymore. Maryanne had looked the house up online while the meatballs were simmering, and there was no record that Patty had ever sold it, but she might have rented it out.

The bereaved mother probably moved away a long time ago. Maryanne hadn't seen her around town in years. She was ready to give up and was just turning to go when the front door opened.

It wasn't Patty, but rather a pretty woman in her forties who eyed Maryanne distrustfully. She seemed ready to slam the door, but her eyes caught on the food that Maryanne held and she paused.

"Hello." Maryanne swallowed and gave the woman a bright smile. "I'm so sorry to bother you. Is this still the Addison house?"

The woman nodded, her expression guarded.

"I brought dinner," Maryanne said weakly. She cleared her throat. "I knew Emily... when we were young. And Ms. Addison. I just wanted to offer my condolences. To... help, bring food, whatever she might need."

The woman seemed to relax, and she opened the door wider. "My name is Kathleen. I'm Patty's caretaker." In a whisper, she continued, "Patty had a bit of a break with reality a long time ago. She isn't really all there anymore. You're welcome to come in and say hello, but don't take it personally if she doesn't recognize you."

"Oh," Maryanne murmured, tempted to hand over the food and run. She steeled herself. "Okay. Thank you."

"And please..." Kathleen glanced over her shoulder and stepped outside, closing the door most of the way behind her. "Don't mention Emily. At least, don't bring up the *news* about Emily. Patty might talk about her like she's just off at a friend's house. The police came last night to tell her... and she understood that well enough. Didn't remember that her daughter's been gone for decades, but took the news of her body being found shoved into a chest at the bottom of the ocean the way any mother would. I don't know why they had to tell her all that. The poor woman was hysterical all night. Finally fell asleep around four. When she woke up, she'd forgotten all about it. There's no reason for her to relive that trauma over and over. It takes its toll on the body, even if her mind manages to blot it out."

Maryanne blinked away tears, her heart breaking for Patty all over again. She nodded. "Of course. I understand. Thank you."

Kathleen pushed the door open and led her first into the kitchen. Aside from a new refrigerator, it was exactly the same as Maryanne remembered it. Pictures of Patty's kids still covered the corkboard on the wall. All of them were faded with age now.

Maryanne's gaze caught on an older picture of Emily with two long braids and a gap-toothed grin. She wore a daisy crown that Maryanne had made for her. Maryanne's heart just about broke in two.

She set the crockpot down and followed Kathleen through to the living room, where Patty was staring blankly at some old TV show.

"Look Patty," said Kathleen, "we have a visitor."

Patty turned slowly to look at Maryanne, and immediately her face lit up. She did remember!

"Jean!" Patty exclaimed, and Maryanne's heart sank. "Do we have bridge today? You told me that the Hendersons canceled."

Maryanne recovered quickly. "No bridge today. I made enough meatballs to feed an army, so I decided to bring some by."

Kathleen muted the TV, and Maryanne joined Patty on the couch.

"That was so thoughtful," Patty said. Her voice was thin and weak. She was the same age as Maryanne's mother, only in her mid-seventies, but she looked ninety. Her pale yellow skin hung from gaunt cheeks. "Emily loves meatballs."

"Yeah." Maryanne cleared her throat and looked helplessly at Kathleen. The caretaker held up a weathered deck of cards and raised her eyebrows. Maryanne looked back to Patty. "We don't have the numbers for bridge, but how about a game of Old Maid before I go?"

"Sure." A haunted look crossed the old woman's face as she glanced at the television. "I'm glad you came. I'm tired of these new shows. It's all so dark these days. Rape and murder. As if those things were entertainment. I don't know how people can watch that sort of thing. It's just a plot point to them, but when I think about how I would feel if it were my girl..."

Behind her, Kathleen grimaced and turned off the television. There was a slightly wild look to Patty's eyes, like a memory trying to surface. Maryanne reached out and took the playing cards.

"Old Maid?" she asked. "Or Crazy Eights?"

Whatever was gnawing at the edges of Patty's thoughts retreated, and she smiled. "You pick."

As Maryanne dealt the cards, the phone rang. Kathleen jumped up to answer it. Maryanne couldn't quite make out the caretaker's words from the next room, but her voice was clipped and curt. Maryanne gave her a questioning look when she walked back in, and Kathleen frowned.

"Reporters," she said shortly. "They've been calling all day."

Patty won the first game and they were midway through the second when the doorbell rang. Kathleen went to get it. Maryanne looked after her, frowning. She hoped that this wasn't a reporter as well. Surely they wouldn't show up to an old woman's house uninvited? Not in Bluebird Bay?

But Kathleen was smiling when she walked back in.

"Look who's here!" she told Patty.

A tall, somber man walked into the room. He had the sort of presence that filled the space, making the average-sized living room feel suddenly small.

"Alex!" Patty exclaimed. A sudden grin lit up her whole face.

He was very handsome, in a gruff sort of way. He looked to be a few years older than Maryanne, approaching sixty. Unlike most of the men she'd known in recent years, Alex was fit. And he still had all of his hair. It was mostly gray, but thick, with a slight wave to it.

He smiled in a sad sort of way and held out a bright bouquet of flowers.

"Hi, Patty. How are you feeling today?"

"Oh, I'm feeling fine, just fine! Two visitors in one day. Just lovely."

"I'll put those flowers in a vase," Kathleen offered. She took them and walked into the kitchen, and Alex leaned over the back of the couch to embrace Patty. He kissed the top of her thin white hair, then straightened and offered his hand to Maryanne.

"I'm Alex."

"Maryanne," she replied, shaking his hand.

Another shadow passed over Patty's face, but it disappeared when she looked back up at Alex.

"Can you stay for a while, sweetheart? Joey and Emily should be home soon."

"Sure." Alex smiled down at her. "I have time."

"Are you staying for lunch?" Maryanne asked. "I brought meatball sandwiches."

"I've never said no to a meatball sub," Alex replied. One side of his mouth flickered upwards in a grin, and he circled around the couch to sit in a chair across from Patty.

Maryanne stood. "I'll just go help Kathleen."

She walked into the kitchen, wondering who this man was and how he knew Patty. A nephew, maybe? Maryanne had always thought that Patty had no family left. It was gratifying to see that she was wrong, but she was curious about how this man fit in.

Not a neighbor. Bluebird Bay was a small town, and Alex was... well, he had a memorable face. Maryanne would recall seeing him around town. She was sure of it.

She didn't have to wonder for long. Kathleen filled her in without Maryanne even having to ask. As they put together a lunch of meatball subs and salad, Kathleen said, "Alex was in the army with Joe. Did you know Patty's son, Joseph?"

Maryanne nodded. "A little."

Kathleen's voice was somber as she continued, "Joseph died just before finishing his tour. He was going to come home and help Patty look for Emily... but he was killed in action.

"Alex was Joseph's commanding officer. He felt terrible about what happened, especially in light of how Patty lost *both* of her children in less than a year. He was in the military for a long time, but he would come and visit her every time he was stateside. And I think he sent money, even from the beginning. At first, it was to help her find Emily, but he still sends money now. Pays my salary, to tell you the truth. Takes care of Patty like she was his own mother. And it's not just the money. He visits more than most sons do. Lives in Maine now, and comes by a couple times a week."

Kathleen lowered her voice and continued, "He just heard about Emily. He put on a brave face for Patty, but you should have seen him at the door. Just gutted by the news. They'd always held out hope that maybe Emily was out there somewhere, alive. An amnesia case, maybe, like in the movies. But this... it's worse than not getting closure at all, I'd think. Knowing that she came to such a gruesome end. It's heartbreaking."

Maryanne just nodded. She had no words. The thought of Emily's body stuffed into a trunk made her sick to her stomach, and she pushed the image away.

She heard the low, pleasant sound of Alex's voice coming from the living room, followed by a thin thread of laughter from Patty. He must be a very good man, to take responsibility for the family like that. Visiting Patty when he returned the first time was one thing. It was only decent. But caring for her for so many years, treating her like his own flesh and blood? That was something else altogether. What an extraordinary man.

Maryanne carried the meatball sandwiches out to the dining table, and Kathleen followed with salad and a pitcher of lemonade. They ate lunch together, not talking much except for some very kind comments regarding the food that Maryanne had made.

After lunch, Patty was clearly exhausted. She looked ready to nod off at the table, so Maryanne and Alex said their goodbyes — both promising to check in soon — and Kathleen walked Patty to her room.

Maryanne and Alex left at the same time, and she was overly aware of his presence, his broad arm just inches from hers as they walked down the front path.

"Did you know Emily?" he asked quietly.

"I did," Maryanne replied. "Quite well."

"I knew her brother. I'm almost glad he's not alive to hear the news." He cleared his throat and paused at the edge of the property, looking off into middle distance.

On a whim, Maryanne said, "It's five o'clock somewhere. Probably in the mid-Atlantic, but... would you like to grab a drink with me? I feel like I need to grieve or vent or... something. Just talk it through, with someone who cares. But I don't know anyone who knew the Addisons like I did."

Alex looked down at her, and a faint smile pulled at the corners of his eyes. "Absolutely."

6

FALLYN

Before she even crawled out of bed that morning, Fallyn had called Gabe to tell him that she wasn't up for a dive that day. Probably just confirming what he had already assumed. She should have told him the day before, but she'd still had it in her head that she might be able to power through and continue with her treasure hunt. Which is exactly what she intended to do. Just... not today.

Gabe had sounded both relieved and exhausted, probably from another sleepless night with his newborn daughter. He had been quick to assure her that she was welcome to rebook and use that payment for another day.

He had also offered her a full refund, but had had demurred. She wasn't ready to give up.

Not yet.

But she wasn't ready to get back in the frigid water, either.

Her whole body felt chilled, and not just from the weather.

She was probably still in shock. Her hands and feet were

colder than they should have been on a mild spring day — and more than once that morning as she got dressed, Fallyn had found herself staring into space for long spans of time before finally snapping out of it and continuing with whatever simple task she had been in the middle of, like brushing her teeth or putting on her thickest pair of socks.

She was familiar with this feeling of full-body lockdown, her mind retreating to a place of blankness, a sort of forced armistice imposed on her waking mind by her nervous system. It was how she had responded to some of her earliest cases, shutting herself up in her room for days at a time, eating Top Ramen and watching black-and-white movies until her body recovered its wits and she was a functioning human being again.

And it was how she had responded to that last case in Chicago, the one that had pushed her over the edge. Only that episode had lasted for weeks, months... it's possible she had never fully recovered from that, or even from the constant stress of her work as an investigative journalist. Maybe that was why this find had hit her so much harder than she'd expected.

She was surprised that her nervous system wasn't completely inured to horror after nearly twenty years of investigating and writing about violent crimes in Chicago. Then again, coming within inches of a corpse at the bottom of the Atlantic was... a novel experience, to say the least.

She had covered more cases than she could count... and her heart still broke for the victims and their families. Every time. It was what had made her so good at her job. And it was why she had to quit.

At least Bluebird Bay was a whole lot easier on her

nervous system than Chicago had been. The day dawned calm and quiet. Small birds squabbled just outside her window, and she could hear the faint sound of waves in the distance.

Her room at the inn was a peaceful, cozy space with handmade quilts and plush rugs. When she didn't go downstairs for breakfast, Molly came tapping at her door with a tray full of crumpets and tea.

"I hope I didn't wake you," Molly said as Fallyn opened the door. "But the day's getting on and these crumpets are just incomparable when they're still hot from the oven. I had to bring you some of this last batch while they were still warm."

"You didn't wake me," Fallyn replied as she took the tray. "Thank you so much."

"And don't feel like you have to eat in your room if you don't want to. But if you want your peace and quiet, I completely understand. Up to you."

Fallyn smiled at the kind innkeeper. "It's been a very long time since I had breakfast in bed."

"You just enjoy yourself, then. I brought you some Earl Gray, but you just give me a ring if you need coffee or more jam or anything else, alright?"

"Earl Gray sounds perfect. Thank you, Molly."

"My pleasure, hon."

Fallyn did her breakfast up right, spreading globs of butter and cream and blueberry jam and marmalade each on their own crumpets (she was in the camp that found mixing butter and jam on the same piece of toast to be utterly repulsive — the same plate was fine, but for all that was holy, not the same *bite*). She drank her tea with plenty of cream and sugar.

It was a far cry from the black coffee and protein bars she had subsisted on for years in Chicago, always on the go at the most obscene hours.

This was a heartening, soul-nourishing breakfast that warmed her to the tips of her toes.

After a leisurely breakfast in bed, Fallyn went for a walk. Just to stretch her legs and admire small-town Maine.

But just a mile into her walk, Fallyn found herself standing in front of the police station she had passed on her way into town. She stood there for a long time, staring up at double doors made of tinted glass.

This was none of her business. She should go back to the inn, take a hot bath, and watch old movies until her nervous system felt fully regulated again.

And she would.

Just as soon as she asked Detective Ethan Jenkins a few questions. He had asked her to come in, after all. She would have a short conversation with the person whose responsibility this actually was, and then she would let it go. For real this time.

Fallyn looked up at the clear blue sky and took a deep breath of the fresh spring air, preparing herself for the noise and chaos of a police station. Then, she marched up the concrete steps and through the doors.

The waiting room was completely empty, save for a middle-aged woman sitting behind the front desk. The place was downright quaint, with plush chairs and magazines. For a moment, she wondered if she had walked into a dentist's office instead of a police station. But as Fallyn walked forward, she realized that the squat, kindly-looking woman behind the desk was in uniform. A police officer.

Fallyn cleared her throat. "Good morning. I'm here to speak to Detective Ethan Jenkins."

"Do you have an appointment?"

"No," Fallyn faltered, "but he did ask me to come in."

"One moment, please."

The woman pressed a button, spoke briefly into the phone, and the detective appeared a moment later.

"Ms. Rappaport," he greeted Fallyn. "Thank you so much for coming down. The conference room is free, if you'd like to come through?"

"Sure." Fallyn followed him down a short hallway and into a rather run-down room with a battered wooden table and plastic-upholstered chairs. He offered her a terrible cup of coffee and sat down across from her. Fallyn used the hot cup of coffee to warm her hands, which had turned chilly again.

"How are you holding up?" he asked. "I can imagine what a terrible shock that must have been, finding a body when you were just out for a dive on vacation."

Fallyn just nodded, unsure of what to say. He didn't seem inclined to pry into *why* Fallyn was diving in Maine in what was possibly the coldest month of the year in terms of water temperature. And she decided to keep it to herself that she had seen countless crime scenes that were far more horrific than a long-dead corpse.

"I pulled all of the files I could find relating to this case," he told her, raking a hand through his hair. "Even brought them home with me last night. There isn't much to them, to tell you the truth. The police work was slapdash. It seems like they did the bare minimum and then just closed the case. There was no sign of a struggle, no boyfriend to interrogate... no suspects at all. She just left one night and never came home. Her car was never found. The cops on the case were quick to decide that she was just another runaway."

"Just like that." Fallyn's voice was dull in her ears, a low monotone.

"There was some friction over curfew at home, and friends of hers told the guys working the case that Emily was always talking about leaving Bluebird Bay to move to Portland or New York City, about breaking out of her shell and getting out of town for good.

"They never really got any good threads to tug on... and honestly, it seems like they were okay with that. I'm not sure if they were quick to give up or if there really weren't any more leads to pursue..."

"What about now?" Fallyn asked, tearing her gaze from the coffee cup in her hands and looking the detective in the eye.

"I'm doing what I can, but there's basically no budget for staff on a case this old." He must have seen something in Fallyn's expression, because one side of his mouth twitched upward in a rueful grin and he said, "I know. I don't like it one bit either. I'm working with the brass to get some leeway, but it's a small department with limited resources. In cases like these, sometimes the squeakiest wheels get the grease... and I know it shouldn't matter, but the victim didn't have much family. Due to her mother's health, she isn't beating down their door demanding answers. No one is."

Fallyn swallowed and looked down. A rapid movement pulled her attention back up; Detective Jenkins was raking a hand through his hair again, looking frustrated. He dropped his arm and met her eyes with a solemn gaze.

"I'm going to do what I can, Ms. Rappaport. But I can only go so far before they yank the leash. Now, if I got some new information, or a lead that hadn't been run down back then, I might be able to get some support..."

Fallyn stared at the detective, and he stared back. With a jolt, she realized that he had found out about her somehow. Heard through the grapevine that she was a reporter, or searched her name online and seen countless articles on crimes like this one.

Was he giving her a hint? Telling her that if *she* decided to poke around, give him something to work with, he would be able to put more resources towards this cold case?

She gave him a questioning look, and he responded with a faint nod and encouraging smile.

"I'm not a reporter anymore," she said quietly.

"No," he said quickly. "I mean, I didn't know that, but— obviously you have no responsibility to— it's not your-" He shook his head and cleared his throat. "Thank you for calling it in and sharing what you found. If I make any progress on the case, I'll let you know."

"I appreciate that."

They stood, and the detective offered Fallyn his hand. She shook it, recognizing that he was a good man in a difficult situation. There wasn't much he could do.

Fallyn walked out of the tiny police station and down the front steps. On the sidewalk, she spared a glance at her watch before remembering that she had postponed today's dive. Without even thinking about it, she began walking towards the library that she had passed on her way to the police station.

It couldn't hurt to have a look through the newspaper archives and see what the local reporters had to say around the time of Emily's disappearance.

7

MARYANNE

They each drove their own vehicle, and Maryanne led the way to her favorite bar and restaurant, a slightly upscale place with polished wooden surfaces and an ocean view. It was quiet at this time of day... but despite the empty tables, Maryanne again had the impression of Alex being too big for the space. It had less to do with his size — the man was tall and well built, but not freakishly so — than it did with the way he held himself. She imagined that he would look more at home in the woods or on a wind-whipped beach than he did in any indoor space.

Not all military men gave that impression... maybe it was the many years that he spent as an officer. He sketched out his career briefly, when Maryanne asked. She told him of her work on various charities.

Once they had drinks in their hands — a martini for Maryanne and a Guinness for Alex — the conversation turned towards the Addisons.

"I remember Patty so differently," Maryanne murmured, toying with the olive at the bottom of her drink. "She was tired sometimes, but even after a ten-hour shift, she was so vibrant and joyful. And *funny*. She had such a great sense of humor. I was just a kid, and I didn't know moms *could* be funny."

"I never knew her then." Alex took a sip of his beer. "I've seen pictures, and of course Joe used to talk about her. About both of them. But by the time I met her, she was alone."

His face clouded over, and Maryanne felt for him. He was clearly affected by the tragedy, just like Maryanne was. If she knew him better, she would reach out and take his hand. Instead, she took a long drink of her martini.

"I wonder if there's anything the police will be able to do," she said, "after all this time."

Alex shook his head and said grimly, "I don't know. But it seems unlikely. I doubt that there was anything in that chest that could identify her killer this many years later. No DNA evidence would survive that long, not in a state that they could test... But what do I know? Technology keeps speeding up to the point that half of it seems like magic to me. Who knows what kinds of tech they have in forensics labs now."

"There's no way Bluebird Bay even has a forensics lab," said Maryanne.

"Portland?" he suggested.

She shrugged. "There must be old files, at least. Records of people they interviewed back when the case was still open... maybe they'll jiggle something loose."

Alex didn't look hopeful. "It's a cold case on a cold trail. I don't think they're going to put much effort into finding out what happened to her."

"I'm friendly with the Sullivan sisters," Maryanne murmured, thinking out loud.

Not friends, exactly, but friendly. They had all been cordial to her ever since she had smoothed things over with Anna and apologized for the way that she had treated her in high school... and for some time afterwards. And after what had happened to her husband, Paul, Steph knew exactly how painful it was to have someone you loved disappear, to wonder what had really happened to them...

Alex frowned in confusion. "Who?"

She shot him an apologetic smile. "Some girls I went to school with. One of them lives with Detective Ethan Jenkins. I could call her — Stephanie — and ask if the police department plans to put any real effort into figuring this out."

"I'd appreciate that." Alex met her eyes, and Maryanne's stomach fluttered. His eyes were a complex mix of olive green and brown and gold, and there was something in them that made her heart race.

She ducked her head. "It's the least I can do."

Alex leaned back and drank his beer, looking out the window at the silver sky and slate-gray ocean. Given this morning's news, she probably could have chosen a better spot for a drink. Maryanne took another sip of her martini and considered what she would say to Stephanie.

She just wanted justice for Emily.

She wanted to know that the man who had done this wasn't still out there doing harm.

Alex leaned towards her, and she looked up with a start.

"I wouldn't share this information with most people," he said quietly, "but I've hired a private investigator to do some digging as well. A local guy named David Shaw. No word just yet, but it's only been a few hours."

"Wow," she breathed. "That's really admirable... I mean,

it's more than most people would do. And for a girl you didn't even know."

Alex looked away again and leaned back in his seat.

"Joe was like a little brother to me," he said slowly. "I... mentored him, I guess you could say. Bonds grow fast and strong when you're in a war zone, together all the time in life-or-death situations. There are times that you *have* to trust the other guys, just because you have no choice. But Joe... Joe was somebody that I could *really* trust. I trusted him to have my back, but more than that, I trusted that he had *everybody's* back. That he would always do what was right." He shook his head and sighed, as if frustrated by the inadequacy of his words.

"If you met Joe, you would understand. He was the best guy I ever knew."

"Tell me about him," she said softly.

"He was this kid from Maine, right?" Alex said with a smile. "The desert heat terrified him. And how did that fear manifest? Not hiding out in the shade or trying to shirk his shifts. Joey spent his off-duty hours going around to everybody who was standing out in the blazing sun, making sure they had enough water. Everyone made fun of him for it... but they loved him for it too.

"Once, we were headed out on a recon job, and Joe volunteered to come. He insisted on coming on that recon job so that Sanchez — this nineteen-year-old kid with clumsy hands and a new baby at home — wouldn't have to go. He was always doing stuff like that. Going above and beyond, doing stuff that he didn't have to do because he was always looking out for everybody else. It's what got him killed, in the end," he finished quietly.

Maryanne clasped her hands together to avoid reaching out to comfort this stranger who didn't *feel* like a stranger. Instead of taking his hand or patting him on the arm, she just said quietly, "He sounds extraordinary. The fact that a man like that chose you to be his role model says something about you, as well."

Alex shrugged off the compliment, but his expression softened. Just a bit.

He waved down a waitress and requested another round of drinks.

"Do you mind if we talk about something else for a while?" he asked when she'd walked away. "Something a little less... heavy?"

Even after a drink, Alex looked tense and on edge. Maryanne was happy to oblige.

"Favorite drink?" she asked as the waitress set down their new drinks.

"Guinness." Alex thanked the waitress and then turned to Maryanne with a smile. He raised his glass in a toast, and clinked it very lightly against the martini that Maryanne held. They both drank.

"Favorite movie?" she asked him.

"Monty Python," he replied immediately. "Any and all. But Holy Grail, if I had to choose."

A surprised smile stretched Maryanne's face. "Really? I would have guessed... I don't know. A Few Good Men, or Born on the Fourth of July or something."

Alex groaned. "No way. No military movies for me. Ever. I like my entertainment to be mindless."

"Aren't knights a kind of soldier?" she teased.

"As terrifying as the white rabbit is," he said with a

straight face, "it's not quite the same thing. What's your favorite movie?"

"Legally Blonde," she said, and Alex smiled. She looked away, embarrassed. "I like Reese Witherspoon. Always have."

"No, it's suitable. The pretty girl who's constantly underestimated."

She looked back at Alex. "You've seen Legally Blonde?"

"I like comedies," he said easily. "It's a good one."

She leaned back, feeling more relaxed after a martini and a half. "How about music?"

"What about it?"

"Favorite bands?"

"Nothing out of the ordinary. The rock bands I grew up listening to. The Rolling Stones, Led Zeppelin, Santana... But I listen to a lot of classical music these days, just to have something on in the background. Movie soundtracks sometimes, like Lord of the Rings or Jurassic Park."

"Lord of the Rings," she repeated, trying and failing to keep a straight face.

Alex's eyes shone with humor. "You heard me. What about you? What do you listen to?"

Maryanne's smile fell. She couldn't remember the last time she had listened to music. "Nothing. I just realized that I don't listen to music anymore. That's so sad."

He raised his eyebrows. "Never?"

Maryanne shook her head. "I'm always listening to... well, to people talking, instead. NPR, audiobooks, that sort of thing. Podcasts, sometimes."

"I like podcasts," he said encouragingly.

"Sure, they're great. But I stopped listening to music without even realizing it." She looked thoughtfully towards the bar. "They have live music here, I think. They used to, at least. I haven't come in ages."

"Well, what sort of music did you used to listen to?"

She grinned, embarrassed. "Funk?"

"Oh," he said, lightly teasing. "You were one of those."

"I loved to dance!" she said, laughing. "Funk bands were the best to dance to. Commodores, Prince... I really loved Average White Band."

"My high school was split down the middle," Alex said. "Rock and funk. So we had two bands at prom. They traded off, nonstop music. It was great."

"What, no punk band?" she teased.

"No punk band," he said with mock solemnity.

"We didn't even have one band," Maryanne pouted. "Just a DJ. Then, when I was in my twenties, the clubs all started playing rap and techno. I feel like I missed out. I'd go see the funk bands, when I could. I loved to dance, but my ex never did. It was way more fun to go out with groups of girlfriends, anyway. Then it was just about the dancing and the music."

"I didn't get to many concerts as a kid — I joined up at eighteen — but I remember this one time..." Alex launched into a story about an obscure band that the military had flown out to perform, and a singer who had passed out from heat stroke mid-song. That led into more stories, and Maryanne was still laughing when a married couple in their eighties walked by their table. She realized that the early-bird dinner crowd was starting to filter in. The sun was low in the sky, and the ocean outside the window was colored a purplish blue.

She couldn't believe how fast time had flown by. Her

stomach rumbled, and she looked longingly at a plate of fried calamari as it passed.

"Dinner hour snuck up on us," Alex said in his wonderfully deep voice. "Seeing as we're already here... would you like to have dinner with me?"

A shock of pleased surprise went through her, and Alex grinned winsomely.

"I bet we can get an early-bird special."

Maryanne returned his smile. She had taken note of his empty ring finger hours ago, but wouldn't have been bold enough to ask him herself. "I would love that. This place makes the most amazing seafood."

"My favorite."

She hid her face behind a menu, even though she already knew what she wanted.

Despite having *bad* luck and choosing bad men, she had never been able to turn off that part of her heart that longed for love.

Maybe she would crash and burn.

Again.

But at least she would go out swinging.

8

FALLYN

Fallyn didn't flake on her next scheduled dive... but the entire time she was out there, she wished that she had. Gabe was kind, but quiet. His face was drawn, with dark shadows under his eyes. How much of that was related to their last gruesome outing and how much of it was simply the result of sleep deprivation, Fallyn had no idea. But it was a quiet ride out of the harbor and over the somewhat choppy water of the gray, frigid Gulf of Maine.

It was a foggy, blustery day, and she was chilled before she even got in the water. She kicked listlessly along the bottom of the sea floor and saw absolutely nothing. It was like being lost in an icy fog, eerie and unsettling. The light was dim, the visibility was terrible, and she was too distracted to really focus on her search.

If Gabe was surprised to see her surface only half an hour after starting her dive, he didn't show it. He brought her back to the marina, making some small effort at conversation, but she sat there in numb silence. When they finally docked, she changed as quick as her numb fingers could manage and drove home — she knew it was silly, but she had already started to think of her cozy room at The Seal Pup as such — on autopilot, squinting against the bright silver sky. Once she had thawed out in a hot bath, her brain started working again... to some degree.

It had been foolish to go out on a dive when she was still recovering from the shock of her last outing. She was trying to ease her overwrought nervous system *out* of freeze mode, and today's plunge into freezing cold water hadn't helped. But she hadn't wanted to flake on Gabe. Every day that she canceled was a day that he could have been out with other clients. She could try canceling and telling him to keep the money rather than rescheduling, but she had a feeling that the honest young man would insist on giving her a refund.

And more than that... she didn't want to give up. It wasn't that the treasure itself was important to her. It was the excitement of the adventure that she was desperate to recoup, that flame of hope that had been snuffed out when her whimsical quest had been marred by a crime scene.

Another crime scene.

Would she never be able to escape that gruesome world?

Was this her karma for years of chasing violence and tragedy? Reporting on the pain and grief of strangers? It's not as if she had ever *committed* a violent crime... but she had built her career on them. Profited from them.

How would she ever wash her soul clean of all of that?

When Fallyn's bath had cooled to room temperature, she climbed out and scrubbed at her skin and hair with one of the inn's fluffy white towels. She pulled on a pair of jeans and a thick sweater. And then, before she could talk herself out of it, she headed for the old Addison place.

She needed to process what she had found. And she didn't want to write about it, didn't even really want to investigate it... but it was what she knew how to do. Maybe she could use her talents for *justice* for once, rather than simply fueling the fear-driven corporate news machine.

Still, when she found herself standing at the front door of a little white house, she second-guessed herself. What right did she have to invade this woman's privacy, her peace?

Fallyn was just turning to walk back to her car when the door opened.

"What do you want?" The woman's voice was measured — unfriendly, but not overly aggressive. Fallyn turned to look at her. She looked close to Fallyn's age, maybe a year or two older — much too young to be Emily's mother.

"I'm sorry to bother you." Fallyn faltered. "I was looking for Patty Addison."

"Why?" the woman asked in a flat tone, looking Fallyn up and down with a closed expression.

Fallyn swallowed. "Does she live here?"

"She's asleep. Why are you looking for her? Are you a reporter?"

"No," Fallyn said hesitantly, unwilling to lie. "I mean, I used to be, but—"

The woman moved to close the door, and Fallyn acted out of reflex. She slid her foot forward, lodging her boot between the weathered front door and its wooden frame. The woman's eyes narrowed, and she stared Fallyn down. Their faces were a scant foot apart from each other. She could see the clumps of mascara on the woman's eyelashes.

"My name is Fallyn. I'm the diver... I'm the one who

found Emily. What was left of her," she added in a voice that was almost inaudible, even to her own ears.

Immediately, the door swung open.

"Oh, you poor thing," said the woman in an entirely different tone. She stepped aside and offered Fallyn admittance into the house. "My name is Kathleen. I take care of Patty. She really is asleep, but she probably won't be for long. Why don't you come in for a cup of tea? Or some hot cider? I just started some going on the stove."

"That sounds wonderful." Relief washed over her at the sudden change in Kathleen's demeanor from guardian to caretaker. "Thank you so much."

Fallyn followed Kathleen through into the kitchen. It was outdated, but cozy and clean and fragrant with the scent of spiced apple cider.

"That smells divine," Fallyn said.

Kathleen smiled. "The secret is orange peel, in addition to the cinnamon and all. It'll be better if I let it simmer a bit longer. Would you like a cup of tea? We have chai or chamomile."

Fallyn gave her a weary smile. "Chamomile, please." She wasn't sure her nerves could take the caffeine today.

"Have a seat. It'll only take a minute."

Fallyn took a seat at the kitchen table and accepted the cup of tea with a grateful smile and a word of thanks. Kathleen even set out a plate of sandwich cookies. Fallyn took one to be polite and found herself immediately reaching for another. They were warm and flavorful with bits of candied ginger, and the crème in the middle was sweet, tart lemon.

Kathleen sat down and wrapped her hands around her

mug of chai. "I can't even imagine how traumatic that must have been for you," she said quietly.

Fallyn shrugged uncomfortably. "It's nothing next to what Patty has suffered."

"True enough," Kathleen murmured. "Sometimes dementia is a blessing."

Fallyn's hand paused in route to the plate of cookies, and she looked at Kathleen in surprise.

"You didn't know?" asked the caretaker. "She's been in and out of reality for a long time now. More out than in, these days. Whether it's a physical ailment or just her mind retreating from the pain, I don't really know... She talks about her kids all the time, but more often than not, she talks about them like they're still alive."

"She lost more than one?" Fallyn's hands returned to the warm cup of chamomile tea, and she took a tentative sip.

Kathleen nodded, her mouth set in a grim line. "She had two kids, a son and a daughter. Her son died overseas, not long after Emily disappeared. A war hero. Not that it takes the sting out, for a mother..."

"No," Fallyn agreed quietly. "No, of course not." Good lord, no wonder the woman was out of touch with reality. It was amazing she had survived at all. Fallyn should never have come here. She should leave Patty Addison to the thin bit of peace she had carved out for herself.

"She is still lucid sometimes," Kathleen said suddenly. Fallyn looked up with a start, and Kathleen looked her in the eye. "More than she lets on, I think. Maybe it's easier to pretend... less painful. But I do think she would understand, if Emily's killer was finally found. If there was justice for her daughter. I think... I think it might bring her some relief."

Fallyn took a deep breath. "I can't promise anything... but I do have a lot of experience with this sort of thing. I can at least try to look into things while I'm here in town. Do you... do you know if there's anything left of Emily's things that might help? Any boxes in storage, or—"

Kathleen stood, and Fallyn stopped speaking.

"Follow me," Kathleen said. She led Fallyn down a short, carpeted hallway and opened a door. Fallyn moved into the doorway and then froze in shock.

It was like a museum. Or a shrine.

They stood staring at the pristinely preserved room of a teenage girl, complete with Alanis Morissette posters on the pale pink walls and a vanity table covered with plastic makeup containers. Everything was covered in dust, but it was a thin layer. The room had been cleaned and cared for, and for a very long time. Fallyn looked to Kathleen, who gave her a small, sorrowful smile.

"In some of her moments of lucidity, I tried to convince Patty to change it. But she flat out refused... just in case Emily ever came home. Patty wanted her to know that she had always held a place for her. That she had never forgotten her, or stopped caring... stopped hoping...

"Those moments of lucidity are very few and far between these days, and she probably wouldn't even miss this stuff if I got rid of it... but I don't have the heart. Emily's room will be here as long as Patty is.

"You're welcome to look at anything inside if you think it might help. I know that's what Patty would want. It's just that Alex... that is, Lieutenant Colonel Orloff has hired a PI to look into things as well."

Fallyn had been looking at a row of Nancy Drew books

that lined a low shelf. Now, she frowned and turned to look at Kathleen. "Who?"

"David Shaw, I think was his name." When Fallyn looked at her blankly, she said, "Oh, you mean Alex? He's... family, basically. The only family that Patty has left. Not blood, but... when her son died, Alex decided that it was his job to look after Patty. And he has, ever since. Another pair of eyes can't hurt. Just please make sure to share anything you find with Alex so that he can pass it along to the private investigator he's hired.

"He's supposed to come by tomorrow, and I want to make sure he has access to all the information. I'll give you his number before you leave, if that's all right? The way I see it, the more people working to get to the truth, the better."

"Sure," Fallyn said, absently. Her eyes were roving again, taking in the details of this room. There was a crocheted blanket on the bed. Socks were scattered across the dusty floorboards beneath the bed, and a sweater was draped over the bedpost. It looked as if Emily might walk in at any moment. The dust was no more than what would gather over a summer at camp or her first semester at college. Fallyn shook her head, pushing the phantom smile of Emily Addison out of her mind.

Kathleen gave her a kindly pat on the shoulder and walked out.

So... she wasn't the only one who wanted justice for Emily Addison. A small bit of the weight that lay on Fallyn's shoulders lifted. She wasn't alone in this.

During the long years of her career, other journalists had been more of an annoyance than anything. They were the competition, trying to get the scoop on the latest stories before she could. But this was entirely different. This was another person who actually cared — who cared enough to hire a private investigator!

Fallyn just hoped that the guy wouldn't feel like she was stepping on his toes. But that worry wasn't enough to cause her to back out of this dusty pink room. She had twenty years of experience with investigative journalism and the nose of a bloodhound. If there was something to find in this room, she would find it.

And honestly? The more she saw of Emily, the more invested she felt.

Fallyn drifted towards a corner with pictures pasted onto the wall. Half of them were of Emily and an older boy who looked just like her — the same doe-like brown eyes and upturned nose. He must be her brother, the one who had been killed overseas. There were pictures of Emily as a baby, held up towards the camera by her mother; Patty glowed with happiness, despite the dark circles under her eyes. A few pictures of Emily with friends, though less than Fallyn might expect in the room of a teenage girl. Other than her brother, there were no pictures of boys or young men.

Fallyn pulled out her phone and took pictures of each of the photos that showed other girls Emily's age. She could compare them to the yearbook photos and track them down to see if anyone was willing to talk. Someone might have information that they were willing to reveal all this time later, something that they might have been reluctant to pass on to Emily's mother or the police in the weeks following her disappearance.

Slowly, methodically, she went through each shelf and drawer. She opened books to see if there were notes hidden between the pages but found only idle doodles. Some of them were actually quite clever, like the hundreds of pages of drawings that Emily had used to turn one corner of her algebra textbook into a cartoon flipbook of a mermaid fleeing and then outwitting a shark, making faces at him through the window of a sunken ship.

There was a whole shoebox full of notes written to Emily from different characters — Barbie and Nancy Drew and Lucy Ricardo. Eventually, they gave way to more serious letters sent from overseas, and Fallyn realized that they were all from Emily's brother, Joe.

Her heart broke for Patty Addison all over again. To lose both of her kind, beautiful children... it was no wonder that she wasn't all there anymore. Who would be?

Fallyn read through the letters quickly, the few from Emily that Joe must have brought back from overseas, but there was nothing of use. No mentions of a boyfriend or anyone skulking around. Just a lonely girl relating the seasonal details of life in Maine and telling her brother how much she missed him.

There was nothing in the drawers but clothes, and Fallyn turned her attention to the vanity. Behind the rows of cheap cosmetics was a wooden jewelry box. Fallyn opened it, and a plastic ballerina popped up. When she turned the key on the side, the ballerina began to twirl in an uneven, lurching fashion to a slow and haunting melody. Fallyn looked through the jewelry in search of some clue — a locket, maybe, or an engraved bracelet, but there was nothing. Just plastic earrings and mood rings and a dolphin pendant.

Fallyn thought back to the mermaid drawings and wondered if Emily's final resting place hadn't been somewhat fitting. Plenty of people wanted to be buried at sea. Not shoved into an undersized chest, of course — the gruesome image of Emily's hand floated up in front of Fallyn's face, and the jewelry box tumbled from her hands. She cursed under her breath and knelt to pick up the bits of plastic and silver that now littered the carpet.

Would Emily be buried? Fallyn wondered. Or would her body be cremated and returned to the sea with respect and dignity?

As Fallyn put the last bits of jewelry back into the box, she noticed a crack in the bottom that hadn't been there before and felt a surge of remorse. Then, she realized that the entire bottom was loose. Still kneeling on the dusty carpet, she pulled off the bottom panel to reveal a hidden compartment. Her breath caught in her chest as a small notebook fell into her hand.

Two words swirled across the cover in purple marker...

Emily's Diary.

9

CEE-CEE

"That smells even more divine than usual," Anna shouted as she tromped down the stairs to the commercial kitchen beneath Cee-cee's Cupcakes. "What magic are you making down there?"

Cee-cee grinned and hugged her baby sister when she reached the bottom of the stairs. Anna made a show of dusting off the flour that the hug left on her shirt; Cee-cee smiled as she handed Anna an apron.

"I've been experimenting with the Tom Kha idea."

"Chicken and mushroom cupcakes?" Anna's tone was deadpan but her eyes sparkled with humor.

"Lemongrass," Cee-cee corrected, bumping Anna's hip with hers. "And coconut."

She picked up one of the gingerbread cupcakes she had just made, still warm from the oven, and frosted it with the coconut-lemongrass concoction she had been working on.

"Try this," she said, handing Anna the cupcake.

"Okay, I give," said Anna with her mouth full. "You were right. This is divine."

Cee-cee licked a glob of frosting from her finger and pursed her lips. "It's not quite good enough for the shop yet. I want to figure out how to get the flavor of those citrus leaves they use, the Thai lime? I put some leaves in a bottle of vodka to see if I can make my own flavoring — and you know that the boozy ones are always a hit at events. But I want to try simmering them in water too, or maybe coconut milk, and working that into the batter... I don't know. I'm still experimenting."

"It's perfect as is," mumbled Anna through another mouthful of cupcake.

Cee-cee smiled and turned to wash her hands at the huge metal sink in the corner. "Wait until you taste the final version. I can get it better, you'll see."

"I believe you. Is that what we're working on today? I thought you said you were too busy to work on new flavors."

"I am, but once I get something in my head, I can't seem to help myself. I'll tweak it more down the road. Right now, we need to finish up some more cakes before lunch. They're nearly cool, just need frosting. Those ginger cakes are actually going to have an apple-cinnamon frosting today; I made it with the last of the apple butter I put up last fall. And the blue ones down there are going to get the tie-dye treatment." She dried her hands and uncovered a bowl of blue frosting. "This is my butterfly pea vanilla frosting — we'll fold in some lemon juice at the last minute to get those pink swirls everybody loves."

"Any chocolate?" Anna asked hopefully.

"Always." Cee-cee grinned. "There's a tray upstairs and more in the oven. And a surprise, just for you two."

"Anybody home?" Steph called. She came trotting lightly

down the stairs, still wearing the yoga pants and fitted shirt that she'd worn to the two classes she had taught that morning. She was glowing.

Cee-cee's heart soared to see both of her sisters so happy. Between that lasting blessing and her children's continued well-being, the Sullivan family was doing better than it had in a long time. Max was living her best life; her bookshop was squeaking by financially, but she loved every minute of running her own business and living with her wonderful boyfriend, Ian. And despite the shock that Gabe had gotten recently when that poor tourist had found Emily's body in a chest on the ocean floor, he was loving life as a new dad. Stephanie's three grown kids were all doing well, and Anna was in a good place with her newfound relatives in Cherry Blossom Point.

The story of Emily Addison was a black cloud over Bluebird Bay, but even that long-ago tragedy only served to reinforce Cee-cee's gratitude and joy. Life was so uncertain. They had to make the most of the good times.

Cee-cee was thriving. Her grandbaby was here. Her family was healthy and happy.

This was the perfect time to celebrate new beginnings with Mick.

"The air in here is practically ambrosial." Steph pulled her sisters into a hug and then swiped an unfrosted ginger cake from the pan and took a huge bite.

"Are you here to help or to eat?" Anna asked as she bit into her second cupcake.

"Both," Steph said lightly, pulling her laptop out of her backpack. "Obviously."

"Lay off the merchandise," Cee-cee laughed as Anna

eyed a tray of orange cupcakes that was still too hot to frost. "I made something special for you two."

She fetched a cake stand that she used for special events and uncovered it with a flourish. Mini cupcakes swirled out from the center, a variety of colors and textures covering the platter in a pinwheel design. She had made half a dozen miniature cakes of each and every flavor combination that she was considering for her wedding cake, including some that she had never made for the shop. And some chocolate varieties, just for her sisters.

"Cake samples," she said as Anna stuffed a whole mini chocolate cupcake into her mouth. Stephanie picked up a pale green one and looked at it quizzically.

"Eucalyptus," Cee-cee said uncertainly. "I'm not sure what I was thinking. It would be covered in white for the wedding cake, maybe peppermint... but it didn't come out quite like I'd hoped."

Steph took a cautious bite. "Oh wow. That's actually really good. I don't know why I'm surprised. They're always good. But you're right, not good enough for your wedding cake."

"Of course, I'm tempted to do orange creamsicle," Cee-cee said slowly, picking up a mini cake of the flavor that she'd created just for Mick, "or peppermint candy cane...but it's springtime. Plus, the more I think about it, the more I want to create something that I've never sold in the shop." She ate the orange cupcake with vanilla frosting and continued, "These over here are honey cakes with lemon icing."

"What's that on top?" Anna asked suspiciously.

"Bee pollen." The small granules, also known as bee bread, ranged in color from pale yellow to dark amber. They were an understated, visually arresting alternative to sprinkles.

"Isn't that healthy?" Anna asked with a disapproving frown. "You know how I feel about trying to sneak healthy stuff into my indulgence foods."

"Yes," Cee-cee chuckled, "they're healthy. And too expensive to use in the shop. But I thought it might be an elegant garnish on a wedding cake, just a few sprinkled lines of it on a pristine cream-colored tower... Or there's this one here, the white chocolate with orange marmalade inside."

Her sisters each took a bite.

"It's good!" Steph said.

"Nope," Anna said. "Rejected."

Steph raised an eyebrow. "I think your body is just telling you you've had enough cupcakes for one sitting." She looked back at Cee-cee. "Because this flavor is really good."

Anna paused with a chocolate cupcake halfway to her mouth. "First of all, white chocolate is an abomination. Like, is it chocolate or is it sickly sweet soap? No one knows. Second of all, they're *mini* cupcakes. You're *supposed* to eat this many." She looked at Cee-cee. "Though I hope you plan to forgo the bridesmaid tradition. I really could go the rest of my life without wearing taffeta again."

Cee-cee laughed. "It's funny you should say that. I was thinking of shirking a lot of traditions."

Stephanie closed her laptop with a groan. "Okey doke, well... there's three hours I'll never get back."

"What? Why?" Cee-cee asked.

"I had a whole array of dresses to choose from, along with a bunch of other, um, traditional ideas. There... may have been a PowerPoint presentation involved."

Anna snorted with laughter and Steph glared at her.

Cee-cee offered Steph a ginger-kumquat cupcake. "I should have warned you."

Anna nodded sagely, her somber expression marked by two different kinds of frosting. "You know Steph. Give her a task and she runs with it for miles."

"I do not," their sister shot back glumly.

"You retired from your veterinary practice and took up yoga for fun, right? To relax? How many classes do you teach per week now?"

Steph ignored the pointed question and took a bite of the miniature cake.

Her eyes widened and she looked back to Cee-cee. "This is the best one yet. What is this? Lemon ginger?"

"Kumquat," Cee-cee said. "I'd love to make something citrusy for Mick, but not the same old orange creamsicle I sell every day. Something new."

"So good," Steph said as Anna snatched up a ginger-kumquat mini cupcake to try.

"I'd still like to see your presentation," Cee-cee said encouragingly. "We don't have to throw *every* tradition out the window."

"I might still want a new dress," Anna coaxed, "even if we're not doing the bridesmaid thing." She grabbed another cupcake and added, "I might *need* a new dress if you don't want me showing up wearing an extra-large, heavy-duty garbage bag."

"You can't wear white to a wedding," said Steph with faux shock.

"It would be a black garbage bag. *Obviously*."

"I saw orange garbage bags at the store the other day,"

Cee-cee said helpfully.

"Not my color," Anna replied. She heaved a theatrical sigh. "I guess we should see that presentation."

Stephanie clapped her hands with glee and then opened up her laptop. Some of her ideas were way too fancy for the simple ceremony that Cee-cee wanted, but some she loved. There was a young mom in town who crafted amazing decorations out of driftwood and sea glass; she even rented them out rather than creating new ones for each event. And their favorite Italian restaurant was available to cater.

"And of course you already have a photographer," Anna said as Steph closed her computer.

"I'd love some pictures," Cee-cee said, "but I don't want you to be distracted all night. I want you to have fun too. We can put disposable cameras on every table so that guests can take candid shots. Those plus just a handful of professional snaps from you will be perfect."

"I *like* taking photos," Anna protested, "and I take a lot less than I used to. I don't mind." Cee-cee opened her mouth to argue, and Anna cut in, "I'll engage! I'll mingle! I'll be sociable, I promise. Just a few shots here and there. I'm more at home with a camera around my neck anyhow."

Cee-cee leaned back and took a bite of a chocolate cupcake. She wasn't actually considering a chocolate wedding cake, but of course they had to be on the menu for a Sullivan sister get-together.

She swallowed the decadent chocolate ganache and said, "I want this wedding and reception to be about... well, just being together. I don't want to stress over staging the perfect, most fancy event. I had that with Nate, and look how that turned out."

"Speaking of the devil, does he know the date is imminent?" asked Anna.

"I'm not sure. I haven't seen him for quite a while. Max says he's busy working, trying to move enough real estate to pay Ian back the money he lent him to settle those debts. So that's good, at least. I don't know if he knows about the wedding, though. Max probably told him."

"Enough Nate talk. When are we taking you shopping for a wedding dress?"

Cee-cee grimaced. "I have no idea where to get one. I don't want a traditional dress. No lace or frills or anything."

"Have you seen the ombré trend?"

"The what?"

"It's a white dress, but they dip the bottom in a vivid color, like purple or cobalt blue. Heck, I have one friend who got married in a bright red dress with ruby slippers. On stage in a theater, with Tibetan prayer flags and Thai food..."

Steph pulled a face. "Whose wedding are you even planning right now?"

Anna just stuck her tongue out at her.

"I want something classic," Cee-cee said, "but not super traditional. If that makes any sense."

"Totally," Steph said. "We'll find your perfect dress. Just tell me which day you want to go shopping and I'll have someone cover my classes. We should talk guest list. How many people, do you think?"

"I'd like to keep it to just family."

"No Eva?" Steph asked in surprise.

"Of course Eva. She's family."

"You really don't want to invite any friends?" Anna asked.

Cee-cee smiled. "You two are my best friends. And that's still a lot of people, between the Sullivan crew and Mick's family... he has a bunch of cousins he was close with growing up who all want to come. I don't want a crazy crowd. I'd rather keep it cozy."

"Good," said Steph, "because the venues you like only do cozy. I'll call around and see if any of them are available on the date you picked. For now," Steph said, giving Anna a gentle shove, "we'll earn our keep. Those cakes must be ready to frost by now."

Cee-cee set to squeezing lemon juice, smiling at her sisters as they frosted cupcakes like pros. How many thousands of cakes had they helped her with, at this point? She was so endlessly grateful to have them in her life.

Cee-cee's phone buzzed, and she paused to check her text messages. It was Mick, checking in about dinner tonight. She responded with her entree of choice from their favorite Indian-food place, and he texted back a thumbs-up and a series of hearts.

Cee-cee had so many things to be grateful for.

And right now, officially beginning her new life with Mick was at the very top of her list.

10

FALLYN

The private investigator's office was literally underground. Fallyn walked down a dark stairwell that was creaky and old fashioned. There was a peeling PI sticker on the frosted glass window beside the name that Kathleen had given her.

David Shaw.

Fallyn paused, swallowing a slightly hysterical laugh that bubbled in her chest. She felt like the leading lady in some mystery movie from the fifties.

I knew the dame was trouble the second she walked in. She had great pins, gams... walking sticks.

She forced down another chuckle. Surviving twenty years as a crime journalist had required a fair amount of gallows humor, and it reared its head at the strangest times. But there was nothing funny about the situation she was in.

After finding Emily Addison's diary the night before, Fallyn had stayed up half the night debating whether she should take it to Detective Jenkins or keep it to herself. The private investigator working the case seemed like a good middle option, someone to talk things through with while she made her decision.

Fallyn knocked on the door and a deep voice called in response, "Come in. It's open."

She turned the knob and walked into the small office.

The man at the desk *looked* like he belonged in some movie from the fifties. He was classically handsome, with a strong jaw and aquiline nose. But this wasn't a black and white movie; his shabby office was brown, with spots of color. His dark hair was free of either shiny product or an old-fashioned hat, and he wore only a pale gray button-up shirt.

And pants. Theoretically. Under his desk.

Fallyn cleared her throat.

"Can I help you?" he asked.

"Mr. Shaw?"

"Yes." He paused and then gestured to her. "Fallyn Rappaport, Pulitzer-winning crime reporter, formerly employed by the Chicago Tribune, and, most impressively, one-time recipient of Mrs. Havrilco's coveted 'Poet of the Year' award in third grade for her poignant rhyme-scheme about the fleeting life of a snowman named Jim. Good to meet you."

She smiled in spite of herself. She had come here to determine whether the man was actually decent at his job and whether sharing what she had found would help. And she had to admit, he was making a good first impression.

"Same."

"Have a seat, Ms. Rappaport."

Fallyn sank into the comfortable chair across from him, her eyes scanning the sparse decorations on the wall behind him. He had graduated from The University of New

England, though a closer look revealed that he had majored in Comparative Literature and Society. She wondered how he had ended up as a PI. Well, she supposed that studying stories for four years was as good a start as anything else. Whether it was private investigations or investigative journalism, it always came down to understanding people. Their motives. Their fears. Their stories.

He was sitting still and patient, waiting for her to speak.

"I got your name from Kathleen," Fallyn explained, "and I wanted to bring you this." She pulled Emily's diary from her bag and set it on Shaw's desk. He sat up straighter, and a spark of interest lit his eyes as he read the front cover.

"Where did you find that?"

"Kathleen let me look through Emily's room. I didn't find much, at first. I thought I might chase down some loose leads, like the girls in the pictures on her walls. See if her high school friends remembered anything that might help. But then I found her diary... it was hidden in a jewelry box, in a secret compartment."

"Well done," he said quietly, lifting the small diary from his desk.

"I didn't have time to read the whole thing," she told him. Most of the pages were full, and she had started at the end, with the events closest to Emily's death. "But I marked a few passages for you that might be useful."

Shaw opened the book to the first of four sticky notes that Fallyn had placed between the pages. She had read it again this morning, several times over, and she could still picture Emily's angled, looping cursive as she watched the PI read the short passage.

Big day at work! Or big night, I guess. Long lines at the pharmacy, mostly the usual boring crowd of old people getting their drugs and middle-school kids buying candy, but TWO guys flirted with me. I felt so popular and pretty, even in my stupid too-big work vest.

First Ricky from school came in and let an old lady go ahead of him so that he could come to MY window. And then he bought a pack of condoms!!! All smiling and stuff. Such a dork. He was totally doing it to show off because there is no way Ricky Young needs condoms. It WAS pretty funny though.

THEN not even an hour later this other guy came in. Tall dark and handsome. He made Ricky look like a goofy kid. This guy was SO good looking and so smooth that I could hardly talk but I am 99% sure HE was flirting with ME. He bought a pack of cigs — the expensive kind — and said, "I haven't seen you around before. Do you work here often?" but it was the WAY he said it that sent shivers up my spine. I told him that I work Thursday through Sunday. I wonder when I'll see him again.

Shaw looked up at her, eyebrows raised. "Two potential suspects in one entry. That's a hell of a lot more than the cops ever had. Not that they were really trying all that hard, as far as I can tell." He jotted down Ricky's name on a yellow legal pad.

"The next one is connected," Fallyn told him.

He turned to the next entry she had marked.

Well I was definitely right about "condom guy". What a stupid, immature way to flirt with somebody. No class. He asked me to the homecoming dance. When I said no, he got in front of me when I was TRYING to walk to class and tried to give me a box of chocolates. I told him that I wasn't interested, and he got so mad. THREW the chocolates into a trashcan and stomped off, which just showed me I made the right choice. I have zero interest in dating someone so childish. Yuck.

"I'll do my due diligence," said Shaw, raising his gray eyes from the notebook to look at Fallyn, "but you don't really think that a Bluebird Bay high school kid shoved Emily's body in a trunk and left her out at sea, do you?"

"Stranger things have happened," Fallyn said darkly. She pushed away memories of cases she had reported on in Chicago, boys who seemed far too young to be perpetuating such terrible violence. But it was nearly an everyday occurrence there, some sort of terrible crime committed by a minor. Guns, knives, even one memorable case with a crossbow... Fallyn steeled herself against images of congealed blood and met David Shaw's eyes. "But there's another suspect. Keep reading."

Shaw turned to the next passage, and Fallyn read Emily's sloppy handwriting upside down. She had nearly memorized each of these entries, so it was easy enough. Fallyn had an excellent memory... which felt more like a curse than a gift these days.

Long time no write! I have been too darn busy to write in my diary but I just had to write it down because I can't tell anybody and I am so excited I could explode. It's OFFICIAL!!! The super-hot guy from the pharmacy is MINE. My Sugar

Bear. I want to shout it from the rooftops, but we're keeping it hush hush for now. It's not like it's illegal or anything - I'm SEVENTEEN, after all. It's not like I'm a baby - but he says people wouldn't understand and I guess he's right. Anyway, it's kind of exciting, sneaking around. I got my first taste of alcohol last night!!! I told Sugar Bear how I always wanted to try a tequila shot like they do in the movies, with the salt and the lime, and so he bought this super expensive bottle and brought the fixings and showed me how to do it. On a ROOFTOP!!! It was so fun!!! And super romantic that he remembered.

I asked Sugar Bear to stay over tonight because Mom went down to Portland to see her cousin but he said it was too soon.

How SWEET is that? He is always so thoughtful.

He gave me RED ROSES yesterday and I felt like I was in a movie. Dreams DO come true.

Shaw glanced up at her, a look of revulsion on his face.

"One more," Fallyn said grimly, and he turned to the final page. It was written the day after Thanksgiving, only one week before Emily disappeared.

Mom made me go to Portland with her for dinner at her cousin's house, which was super lame. I was the only one there under forty and everyone wants to hear about school and if I'm going to college, and I just have to smile and pretend when really all I can think about is my Sugar Bear and when I'll get to see him again.

Last weekend was pure magic.

I can't believe I missed out on a long weekend with my Sugar Bear for TOFU TURKEY.

Gross. Mom's cousins are so weird. I've been puking up their frankenfood all morning.

I know Mom would like Sugar Bear if she met him because he is so smart and so wonderful to me, but he's still not ready. He's so sweet and shy. He was patient with me, so I have to be patient with him too. I wish he could meet my friends, at least, or I could see where he lives... but he always says it's too soon. Oh well. I don't mind keeping him to myself a while longer. And he's worth the wait.

The entry, the last that Emily had ever made, ended with a series of purple hearts.

Shaw closed the diary and let out a low whistle.

"Initial thoughts?" Fallyn murmured.

The PI shrugged. "I can start with Ricky Young, because we have an actual name. Finding out who the second guy was will be trickier... but if they were both hanging around at the same time, maybe this Ricky kid saw an older guy talking to Emily a lot. It's worth a shot — and it's the best lead I've got right now. Thank you."

"They both have a potential motive." Fallyn was stating the obvious, but she found that she was reluctant to leave. It was such a relief to have someone to talk to about this. "The boy who got rejected and the man who wanted to keep their relationship a secret."

"I really appreciate you sharing this with me." Shaw paused, seeming to consider his next words carefully. "I understand that you don't owe me anything — you don't even owe Emily's family anything — but if you wanted to work on this together... your experience as a journalist would be a huge help. We have different specialties. I'm good at tailing people. I have good instincts. But I can be kind of... gruff. Not like you. You must have done thousands of interviews over the years."

Fallyn nodded. "Yeah, probably. More than I can count, anyway." She pushed away memories of tearful interviews and doors slamming in her face.

"I read some of your old articles," Shaw said, smiling. His expression turned serious again when he said, "You obviously have a way with people... coaxing information out of them. I'm good at finding information, but... less good at talking to people. They tend to clam up. If you're up for it, I would appreciate your help on this case."

It was exactly the proposal that she had wanted to make to him, but she had been nervous that he would tell her to stay out of it. Of course, she thought wryly, why would he refuse free help at his day job? Not that it was actually *day*... she glanced at the small street-level windows high in the wall. The streetlights had turned on, and their light glistened off of puddles on the pavement.

"I didn't ask for this," she said slowly, "but I'm in it now. I want to find justice for Emily. Some peace of mind for Patty, if that's even possible."

"You're a good woman, Fallyn Rappaport," Shaw said.

She met his ocean-gray eyes with a self-conscious smile. "I have a lot of bad karma to work off, is all."

His expression turned somber and he nodded. There was a look of understanding in his eyes.

"I'd like to keep the diary," she told him, "if you don't mind. I didn't get around to reading the first third of it. I can make copies if you'd like, so we don't have to pass it back and forth?" She also felt like she would sleep better if the diary was returned to its place in Emily's room, and they *both* worked off of the photocopies that she planned to make the next day... but she felt silly saying that out loud in this shabby underground office.

"I would appreciate that. In the meantime, I'll look into Ricky Young and see if he's still around. If so, I'll try to set up a meeting."

"Do you think we should share this with the police?" Fallyn asked quietly.

"You do what you think is right. But no, I don't think so. At least, not yet. They're not going to do anything, not off of what you've found so far. You don't want it ending up in the bowels of the evidence room, gathering dust."

"No," she agreed, thinking back to Emily's dusty pink room. "I don't."

"And if you change your mind, if we find more evidence that might convince them to act, we can bring it all in later. She's been dead for twenty-five years, Ms. Rappaport. Another few days won't make a difference."

Shaw stood, and Fallyn did the same. She was surprised by how tall he was. He seemed too big for this little office, and she wondered again how he had ended up here. Shaw offered her his hand, and she shook it. His grip was strong and steady.

As Fallyn made her way back up the damp concrete steps outside, ninety percent of her brain was focused on the mystery of Emily Addison's death.

And the other ten percent? Was still back in that room with David Shaw.

11

CEE-CEE

The bell over the front door jingled as Mick walked in and maneuvered around the long line of people waiting to order. He shot Cee-cee a grin and walked over to where she stood at the espresso machine.

"Ready for lunch?" he asked.

"Yes," she said emphatically, and Mick's grin broadened. The cupcake shop was packed with its usual lunch rush, but she had brought in an extra employee to cover for her so that she could step out for a lunch date with Mick. They'd spent so little time together lately, each focused on running their own business.

Even today's lunch date was business, of a sort. They were headed to Monzano's to sample a variety of different options for their wedding menu, which would be catered by their favorite Italian restaurant. So... not exactly the most relaxing lunchtime escape. But hey, great food and some time with her adoring fiancé? That was plenty good enough for Cee-cee.

She finished up the latte she was working on and

removed her Cee-cee's Cupcakes apron. With a grateful glance at her well-trained and trusted staff, she and her handsome husband-to-be were out the door for a long lunch.

She looked around when they stepped outside, but Mick's truck was nowhere in sight. Every parking spot was occupied, and she wondered how far away he'd had to park. She gave him a questioning look, and he smiled.

"I knew this street would be jam-packed with your lunch crowd, so I parked at Monzano's. I needed the walk, and look how gorgeous it is out here."

Cee-cee looked up at the pale blue sky and took a deep breath of the cool spring air. When she looked back at Mick, he had his arm offered out to her like a proper gentleman. She grinned and threaded her arm through his to walk the mile to the restaurant. Thank goodness her days of toe-pinching stilettos were behind her. The cushy sneakers that she wore through her long mornings at the bakery were perfect for a walk through town.

The stress melted out of Cee-cee's muscles as she walked down the street arm in arm with Mick. It was a pleasure to know that Cee-cee's Cupcakes was bustling along without her, at least for today. She wanted to shift more towards a managerial role, coming up with new cupcake recipes and running things without putting in the seventy-hour workweeks that she'd grown accustomed to since starting her own business, but she hadn't made that happen yet. Still, she was getting closer.

"I'm so grateful for my staff," she said. "It's a wonderful feeling to be able to hand the business off to them and know that everything will run smoothly. I should do this more often."

"Agreed," Mick said in a hearty tone. "Maybe we'll even get away for a honeymoon? Nothing crazy... but a few days away? A cabin on a lake, long hikes and nights in front of a fire? Or some city decadence? Gourmet food and a show? Whatever you want."

"That does sound lovely," Cee-cee agreed. "But you've been so busy. Would you be able to take the time off?"

"We do have a lot of projects going right now," Mick admitted, "but I trust Jeff to keep working while I'm away, especially if I have time to prepare him and set him up for success. There's plenty of menial work that he can do on his own... and some of the more advanced stuff, too. He's fast becoming a great carpenter in his own right. He knew a fair amount already, and he learns quicker than any apprentice I've had in the past. He's a natural."

"I'm so glad you took him on." Cee-cee squeezed Mick's arm. "He was so lost for a moment there, after his dad... You letting him into your life and saving the day meant the world to all of us. You changed the course of his life."

"I think he would have found his way with or without me," Mick said modestly, "but I'm glad I could help. And I'm glad *for* the help. He's the reason I've been able to take on this extra work. Though I want to slow down a little bit. Have more time to spend with my beautiful bride."

They were at Monzano's before she knew it, and Cee-cee was almost sorry to end their walk so soon. But she was also very hungry, and her stomach rumbled when she caught the ambrosial scent of garlic butter wafting out from the restaurant kitchen.

A server showed them to a corner booth near the kitchen and brought them one small plate after another. Some of the offerings were on the menu, and others were exclusive to the catering side of their business. They mowed through a fennel salad with mandarin segments, a bruschetta board, fresh burrata cheese, a calamari antipasto, and seared scallops. All of them were absolutely delicious. And that was just the appetizers.

"What do you think?" Mick asked as they polished off the last of the small plates.

"It was all wonderful," Cee-cee said slowly, using the last scallop to scoop up the delectable sauce that decorated the small white plate, "but I'd like to keep it simple. A big burrata platter with tomatoes and basil, maybe, or the bruschetta board... I want food that encourages people to mingle, not fussy fare that has people stranded at separate tables. I always thought that assigned seating at weddings was ridiculous."

"I agree wholeheartedly." Mick paused to kiss Cee-cee on the cheek, and she felt her face warm with a blush of pleasure. "Homey, simple summer fair. Family style."

As he said that, a server came out with two dishes of seafood pasta that included clams still in their shells, drowning in a creamy seafood broth, and Mick shot Cee-cee an amused look. Delicious, yes, but not quite what they were going for. Still, they enjoyed the sumptuous food while the sommelier hovered near their table, offering a choice of wine pairings that they could serve with dinner.

"Something less saucy?" Cee-cee murmured when the sommelier went off to fetch more wine.

"Same food, less sauce," Mick agreed. "Like a clambake? Lobster bake? Maybe something really rustic, like a big pot of shellfish in the middle of the table. Or a pile of crab legs."

Cee-cee grinned and said, "Every guest gets a personalized lobster bib."

They both laughed and Mick said, "Okay, something less messy. Lobster ravioli? Shrimp?" He slumped backwards in a display of defeat as their server delivered a bowl of lobster risotto. "I give up. Seafood and Italian food are both inherently messy."

Cee-cee pulled him in for a kiss before helping herself to the aromatic risotto. "Messy's okay. I just don't want it to feel formal and fussy."

"Lobster mac-and-cheese?" Mick suggested.

"Yes! A boatload. And grilled asparagus," Cee-cee murmured, reading over the menu again. "Shrimp, caprese, stuffed mushrooms... lasagna?"

"That all sounds wonderful. Honestly, I'd be happy with literally anything that they make here."

Cee-cee looked up and met his eyes. "You're easy to please."

"To the contrary," Mick said, taking her hand. "I'm very, very picky."

Cee-cee blushed and made a show of hiding behind her menu. When she peered at Mick over the top of the paper, he gave her a smile of pure adoration.

They took their time with the rest of the meal, fully enjoying themselves, and eventually the catering staff came out to discuss their decisions for their wedding menu.

When Cee-cee described what they wanted, Monzano's head caterer was immediately onboard. She helped them choose a simple color scheme with unbleached linen napkins and durable plates. This was a celebration! They would keep things easy and comfortable.

Just as things had been between her and Mick for the entirety of their relationship.

They finalized the menu — which would include boozy tiramisu in addition to whatever Cee-cee devised for their wedding cake — and walked out the door hand in hand. Cee-cee turned towards the cupcake shop, but Mick pulled her towards his truck.

"You're coming with me," he said playfully.

"You're going the opposite direction," she replied. "I can walk back to work. I don't mind. I really enjoyed our walk here. It's so beautiful today."

"I agree! Which is why we're playing hooky the rest of the day."

Cee-cee laughed. "That sounds like a blast, but I should get back to work."

Mick's grip on her hand didn't let up. "Nope! I spoke to your staff yesterday, and you're covered. They'll close up and get everything prepped for tomorrow. I also took the afternoon off. There are hiking clothes in the car and a picnic dinner for the turnaround point. I even packed a bottle of wine. I am whisking you away to spend this gorgeous afternoon outside. Together. Just you and me." He grinned wickedly. "That lunch was business. It doesn't count."

Cee-cee stepped in and embraced him. "My hero."

He wrapped his arms around her and held her tight. In a more serious tone, Mick said, "We've both been so busy lately. You're downstairs baking at four in the morning and I'm working through dinner more often than not... I miss you." He leaned back, just enough to look into her eyes. "*You* are my priority, Cee-cee. You and me, the life we're building together. And our businesses support that, but I won't let them eclipse it. I want to prioritize spending time together away from work."

"I want that too," she said warmly, stepping back to take his hand again. "Let's go."

They turned to walk towards Mick's truck — and nearly ran into Nate. Cee-cee's ex-husband was walking towards Monzano's with his head down, typing busily into his phone. He looked up with a start, and his face blanched when he registered Cee-cee and Mick.

"Celia. Hi. Didn't see you there."

He looked bad. Frazzled and red-eyed. Before Cee-cee could even reply, his eyes flicked back to his phone and he edged towards the building.

"Hi Nate," she said uncertainly.

"Lunch hour," he muttered. He glanced up at her and forced a smile. "Gotta run. Need to be back in the office soon. Good to see you."

"Yeah, okay. Bye," Cee-cee said to his back as he scurried away.

How bizarre. For the vast majority of the decades that they lived together, Nate was always perfectly poised and polished.

Was he drowning in debt again? Why did he look so stressed and haggard?

To see him like this was deeply disturbing, and her heart broke for her kids. They might not always like or respect their father, but he was a part of them. They loved him deeply, and they worried for him when they should be focused on their own lives. Max was building her business, and had authors coming in every weekend for readings and book signings, and Ian's escape room business was thriving, even in the off season. And Gabe had so much on his plate, between running a small business and recovering from the stress of finding that corpse in the Gulf. Gracie was perfect, but life as new parents for Gabe and Sasha was a huge adjustment. It was inherently exhausting.

They all had enough to worry about without adding Nate to the list.

"Nope," Mick said gently, taking her by the arm and steering her away from the restaurant. "Don't do it. This isn't your problem, Cee-cee. Whatever is going on with Nate is for *him* to lose sleep over, not you. You can't heal the whole world. You're not responsible for him."

"I know. You're right. I just worry about the kids' lives being disrupted."

"They aren't kids anymore, my love. Gabe is a father, and Max is a successful business owner. They both have great partners and an amazing mother and doting aunts. They'll be okay."

Cee-cee looked up at her fiancé and let the love in his eyes steady her. "You're right."

They began to walk across the parking lot, and he said, "Besides, my guess? He knows we're getting married and the ship he's imagined boarding with you again has finally sailed. I'd be having sleepless nights if I was him, too."

She nodded. Her ex-husband *had* made a couple of weak plays for her over the past year. That's probably all she was picking up on — his usual workday stress coupled with the stress of running into his ex-wife and her husband-to-be.

Cee-cee made a mental note to casually ask her daughter how the repayment plan was going for the loan that Ian had given Nate. But for now, she pushed her worries aside.

She wanted to focus on the wonderful afternoon ahead with her fiancé.

Things were coming up roses for them right now, and she had everything that she'd ever wanted. Her kids were happy and thriving. Her sisters were healthy and lucky in love. She had a successful business that brought joy to her community. Her baby granddaughter was perfect and loved.

And to top it all off, she was about to marry the love of her life. The most wonderful man she knew. She was the luckiest woman in the world, and she knew it.

In fact, she was almost painfully aware of it — and of how quickly things could change. It was only a matter of time before the cycle moved and shifted. She had to enjoy it all while the sun was shining on the Sullivan family.

Mick opened the passenger-side door for Cee-cee, and she kissed him full on the lips before climbing into his truck.

"Let's get hiking."

12

FALLYN

Fallyn ate breakfast in her room at the inn and spent the morning rereading Emily's diary entries. She had photocopied them all and dropped them off at the private investigator's office the day before; while she was there, Shaw had invited her to accompany him when he went to speak to Richard Young. She would head over to his office soon, and they would drive to Young's house together.

Fallyn was more than happy to help him find information that would help bring Emily's case to a close. The truth was, she had grown fond of the girl. The entries that she had shared with Shaw, the frazzled scratchings of a lovesick teen, didn't do justice to the person she had been.

She brushed the crumbs of her breakfast from her fingers and opened the diary again to one of the earliest entries. It was written to Emily's brother, Joseph.

Dear Joseph,
I just finished writing you a letter that's all sunshine.

Mom's new job and all the A's I pulled in this month. You're too far away for me to tell you what's really going on... so I'll write it here.

I CAN'T BELIEVE you signed on for a second tour. Sometimes I hate you for leaving. You could have gone to college in Portland or gotten a job here in town, but instead you had to go and be a hero on the other side of the world. And I don't understand why you had to leave us. AGAIN.

Mom's broken, Joey. She's so worried about you. She tries to smile, but it falls right off her face the second she thinks I'm not looking. She's just working and working all the time, probably so she doesn't have to think about you. And I'm just here, all alone in the house with my stupid math homework. It's the worst. I don't get why anyone would ever want to live alone.

Our family is broken. We don't know how to be a family without you. I have nightmares about you coming home in a box, and when I go to the kitchen at two in the morning to make myself a cup of tea, mom is already in there.

We miss you so much.

Remember that puppy we found when you were ten? It was stuck down in that creek and you wouldn't wait for Bobby to come back with help. You didn't think the mutt would last that long, and so you went down to get it yourself. Just about drowned in the process, but you did it. Only for Bobby to get to keep it because mom's allergic. You didn't even mind.

If you would do that for a dumb dog, I can only imagine what sort of danger you get into over there. What you'd do for one of your fellow soldiers, or for a kid.

Don't be a hero, Joe. Please. Just come home.

Fallyn flipped forward to a happier entry.

Happy birthday to me!! I am sixteen today and I never could have ever guessed what Mom would get me as a birthday present. She got me a CAR!!! She says Joe chipped in half the money and I just finished writing him a sappy thank you letter. I'm going to put in a picture of me and the car before I send it.

I NEVER thought I would be the kid to get a car for her sixteenth birthday. But Mom knew how much I wanted one, and she knew how brokenhearted I've been, stuck at home without Joe or Maryanne, who never comes around anymore now that she got married.

It turns out that Mom's been working crazy hours to save up for my birthday present! So that's a doubly happy surprise — I have a car for when mom's working AND she'll be around more now that she doesn't need to work so many hours. I almost told her I would rather have her home than have a car... but I just said thank you. It makes me want to cry that she would do this for me, and I can't even tell if they're happy tears or sad.

The car is kind of old and funny looking, with this boxy face in front, but the person who had it before me took really good care of it. It's called a Volkswagen Rabbit, and it's Candy Apple Red!! without a scratch or a dent, even though it's almost as old as I am. It's got personality, that's for sure. I love it. Her? Feels like a her. I suppose she needs a name. One will come to me once I get to know her better. I can't believe that she's mine!

My own car!! I'm going to drive to the beach every day,

even when it's freezing cold I can just sit in my car — MY car — and look at the waves.

Someday I'll drive right out of this ice-cold state, all the way south.

I just grin like a fool every time I look at her, because to me she looks like freedom.

Fallyn closed the diary with a sigh and glanced at her watch. It was nearly time to meet David Shaw; they would drive to Young's house together and see whether the guy who was interested in Emily back in high school was a solid lead or a dead end.

Richard Young lived in a huge white house on the outskirts of Bluebird Bay. The hedges were perfect rectangles, and there was a Mercedes parked in the driveway.

"You're sure this is the right Ricky Young?" Fallyn asked as Shaw parked the car.

"I'm sure," he replied.

That was it. No bluster about how he did this for a living. No snide comment or sideways glance. Just... steadiness. A calm confidence.

"What do you know about the guy?" she asked.

"He works for a pharmaceutical company. Never married. That's about all I could find. Not much of an online presence. Shows up on social media a few times a month to argue with old classmates or correct his cousins' typos, but doesn't post anything of his own besides the occasional picture of his car."

"Charming," Fallyn said under her breath.

Shaw flashed her a look of amusement before climbing

out of the car. They walked side by side up the wide, straight path that led to the front door. Shaw gave the door a sure, firm knock — and it was only a few seconds before Ricky opened it.

"I was wondering how long it'd take until you showed up," he said by way of greeting. Ricky looked Fallyn up and down and then turned back to Shaw. "Not bad. I was thinking it would take at least another day or two. You're obviously more diligent than the detectives who worked the case all those years ago. Come on in and let's get this over with."

He turned and walked away, leaving the front door open. Fallyn glanced at Shaw; that faint look of amusement came over his face again, softening the hard line of his jaw.

"He thinks we're cops," Shaw murmured, his voice so low that Fallyn read his lips more than hearing the words.

She flashed him a wicked grin. "I'm in no hurry to disabuse him of that notion."

Shaw walked inside and Fallyn followed, closing the front door behind them. The house was clean and neat in the way that the homes of the rich and lonely often were. The living room in which Ricky stood waiting for them was lined with wall-to-wall bookshelves; from what Fallyn could see, the books were organized first by subject and then by author. Most of the books were about science, particularly biology. There was a full shelf dedicated to cosmology and another devoted to robotics and artificial intelligence.

Richard Young was a man who was *very* taken with his own intellect.

"Go ahead and sit down," Ricky said grudgingly. He

slumped into an armchair that looked like it cost more than Shaw's car, and they sat on the leather sofa across from him.

"May I record this conversation?" Fallyn asked, pulling a small device from her pocket.

"Fine by me." Ricky seemed to be trying for an air of generous nonchalance, but there was a childish petulance just below the surface. And beneath that — fear. He swallowed, eyes flicking between Fallyn and Shaw. "Can I get you something to drink?"

"We don't drink on the job," Shaw rumbled. Fallyn bit back a smile.

"Right. Of course. I meant... water?"

"No, thank you," Fallyn said softly.

She was practiced at this, donning kid gloves to handle witnesses who scared easily. There was a pathetic fragility to this man, just beneath his bravado. There usually was. Fallyn could see him as a blustering teenager who purchased condoms from his crush in a bizarre attempt at courtship.

Fallyn pressed record, set the device on Ricky's glass coffee table, and asked: "Why were you so certain we would show up?"

Ricky shrugged and glanced away. "It was public knowledge that I harbored an unrequited crush on Emily Addison. When we were seventeen, I asked her to the school dance with this big romantic gesture. Boombox, rose petals, the whole romantic comedy schtick. A public display of affection, you know? And she turned me down in front of everyone. So of course, people still associate my name with hers. I mean, she disappeared that same semester... I expected that you'd want to cross my name off your list, do your due diligence. I always thought it was pretty pathetic that the cops never asked me any questions when she went missing in the first place."

"It does shine a spotlight on you as a potential suspect," Fallyn said cautiously.

Ricky gave her a long, cold look. When he spoke, his voice dripped with disdain. "I'm aware."

When he didn't say anything more, Fallyn told him, "We need some more information to clear this all up, and find out who *did* want to hurt Emily. Maybe you could start by telling us why you didn't?"

"Why would I?" Ricky snorted. "What's the logic there? Was she gonna go to the dance with me if she was dead?"

"Rejection is a powerful motivator," she said, "and Emily rejected you more than once."

"I had a bright future," he scoffed. "As you can see." He paused to gesture around him, at his opulently furnished house. "I wasn't going to risk throwing that all away on revenge. I'm not an idiot."

Shaw shifted in his seat, looking impatient. "Do you have any information that could help us? People she spent time with before she disappeared? Anyone who was hanging around her?"

"Way ahead of you." Ricky jumped up and came back with a notebook. He ripped a page out of it and handed it to Shaw. Shaw read it quickly and handed it to Fallyn.

It was a list of names; Fallyn recognized some of them from the high school yearbooks she had looked through. Next to each name was a note about how each person was connected to Emily: coworkers, a neighbor, a lab partner from her chemistry class. None of them lined up with what they knew of "Sugar Bear", but maybe one of *them* had seen an older man hanging around Emily. It was something.

"Thank you," Fallyn said when she looked up from the paper.

He sat down again and crossed his arms, wearing a self-satisfied expression. "I've listed them in order based on the probability that they'll have any information."

"That was very thoughtful of you," Fallyn said, just to have something to say. She was certain that Richard Young hadn't killed Emily Addison. She'd felt sure of it from the moment he'd opened the door. This man simply didn't have what it took to kill someone, much less stuff their body in a trunk and dump it into the Gulf of Maine. Even if he had, he would have gone for something like poison. After that, he was more the vat-of-acid type, or at least a deep-woods burial with a sapling on top.

Shaw stood, and Fallyn followed suit. He walked out without so much as a goodbye, and she looked back at Ricky.

"Thank you for your cooperation," she said, picking her recording device up off of his table and pressing *stop*.

"You'll be in touch?" Ricky asked.

"Sure," she lied.

Shaw was waiting for her outside. He opened the car door for her, then circled around and climbed in.

"It wasn't him," they said in tandem, in the same disgruntled tone, and Fallyn laughed.

Shaw gave her a wry look. "I almost wish it was."

"Same." Fallyn grinned, but the smile fell from her face as she looked down at the list of names.

"Theresa Chadwick," she murmured as one of the last

names on the list caught her eye. "She was Emily's friend. She mentions her in the diary more than once."

Shaw nodded as he turned the key in the ignition. "I noticed that too. But we'll go through every name on the list. You never know — the person who saw her the least might be the one who recognized the creep who was hanging around with the teenage girl."

"Back to the office?" Fallyn asked. They had left her car there.

Shaw nodded. He was clearly as eager as she was to track down these names and find out where they lived now. All Fallyn could do was wait. She looked out the window, not paying any real attention to the dreary landscape of Maine before its true flush of spring. After a while, Shaw cleared his throat. She blinked herself out of a daze and turned back to him.

"I'm getting paid by the hour to do this," he said quietly. "Why are you doing it?"

"Why does anyone do anything?" she murmured, looking back out at the skeletal trees that lined the road. She wasn't being deliberately evasive. She just wasn't sure how to answer his question. But she wanted to. She *needed* to — not for him, but for herself.

Shaw was a patient man. He sat quietly while she considered his question.

"Old habits, I suppose," she said at last. "The real question is why I got into crime journalism in the first place. I've asked myself that question a thousand times this past year.

"I grew up in Springfield. When I was in high school, a classmate of mine disappeared. Just vanished into thin air.

No one ever found out what happened to her. Not a runaway — at least, not the sort of kid who you'd think would run away. Her family had money, and they seemed happy enough. She got good grades, had a good boyfriend, was headed for college... We weren't super good friends, but I knew her well enough. One of those kids who had been in school with me since kindergarten, you know?

"And then she was gone. Just this unsolved mystery that no one could figure out. No one ever did. And it hung over all of us, the whole town... but it really stayed with me. Why *me* in particular, I couldn't tell you. I've always been a little... different. *Other*, in a way that I could never quite put my finger on. Could never fix. I was that kid in the corner with a five-pound book, you know?

"Anyway, I went through a phase of wanting to be a detective or join the FBI or something. Even applied to the local police academy. But my dad was a journalist, and he pushed for me to go to a 'real' college instead. So I did, I caved... and I ended up studying journalism. It was the path of least resistance, I guess? And I was good at it. But I never got rid of that investigative itch... the only thing that satisfied it was crime journalism. It was like this gruesome game, hunting down the answers before the cops could. I was good at that too."

Fallyn shook her head. It was a part of her. She didn't *want* it to be, but it was.

"I was trying to figure out how to do something else..." she said slowly. "*Be* something else. And on the first day of my grand new adventure... I found Emily. Her body, anyway. It's like some sick cosmic joke. But I can't walk away now. I just can't. It would eat away at me forever, the not knowing."

Shaw had listened patiently, nodding along. Fallyn cleared her throat, suddenly self-conscious. "How about you? How did you end up a private detective?"

"The money and the glory," Shaw said, deadpan.

His phone rang then, and he paused at a stop sign to check the screen.

"It's my client. I need to take this."

"Of course."

Shaw put the call on speaker and set his phone on the dashboard before tapping the gas pedal again. "Hello, Alex."

"Any developments?"

"Just spoke to the kid who had a crush on Emily. It was a dead end, but he did write up a list of names. Potential leads. I'm headed back to the office to chase them down."

"What about that woman who found her?"

The side of Shaw's mouth twitched as he glanced at Fallyn. "A complete nuisance," he muttered warmly. "Very distracting."

"What was that?"

Shaw continued at a normal volume: "The journalist who found her—"

"Former journalist," Fallyn muttered.

"—came with me to interview Richard Young. She's been very helpful."

"I'll take all the help we can get," said Alex.

He glanced at Fallyn, and she grinned. So Ricky wasn't the killer. At least they'd gotten some leads, and now she had the blessing of Shaw's client to keep working with him. They hadn't gotten far yet, but it felt promising.

Is this what it would have been like?

To work at a precinct? To have a partner? To be part of something bigger than herself?

For the umpteenth time, Fallyn wished that she had chosen differently.

But for the first time, the thought wasn't heavy with despair.

It was full of hope.

13

ANNA

"Do you think Cee-cee's figured it out yet?" Anna asked as she lined up jars of marmalade on the counter.

"Probably," Steph laughed.

They had done their best to keep this surprise wedding shower a secret — they even had Todd and Jeff on pickup duty, ferrying guests to Steph's house from a park down the street so that the cars wouldn't give them away — but it was tough to keep anything from their big sister for long.

Steph pulled a tray of rolls from the oven while Anna put the finishing touches on the hors d'oeuvres platters she had made. They were inspired by Gayle's creations — and while these weren't quite as impressive as the epic platters that the eldest Merrill sister made, they were pretty close. Anna had chosen all of Cee-cee's favorite snacks: prosciutto, swiss cheese, peppery salami, garlic-stuffed green olives, and dried apricots. Best of all, there had been no cooking involved. Just some artistic arranging of different colors. That, she could handle.

Steph had contributed shrimp puffs and other baked

goodies (and her house as a venue), and they were well stocked with all kinds of wine — including plenty of champagne.

"She doesn't know," Anna insisted, trying to convince herself. "How could she? You invited her over for dinner. Nothing unusual about that."

"And you invited twenty other people," Steph said with a smile.

"All sworn to secrecy!"

"What are the chances that not one of them let something slip? I don't think there's a single person in Bluebird Bay who doesn't stop by Cee-cee's Cupcakes at least once a week. She knows all and sees all." Steph intoned this last line dramatically, and Anna snorted.

Jeff arrived with his first pickup, and Max and Sasha walked in.

"I'm sorry we're late!" Sasha said immediately, her voice hushed as she shifted her sleeping baby on her shoulder. "Getting the car seat into Jeff's car took longer than I thought it would."

"You're not late," Anna told her as she hugged Sasha and then Max. "You're the first ones here."

"Yeah, but we wanted to get here early enough to help."

"You just sit back and relax," Steph told her. "Can I get you something to drink?"

"I'd love some water," Sasha replied as Max uncorked a bottle of wine. "I forgot mine in the car."

"Of course." Steph poured her a glass of water and popped in a lemon slice as Sasha perched on a kitchen stool.

"Thank you." Sasha drained the whole glass in one go. "I'm thirsty all the time."

"Breastfeeding will do that," Steph said. "You know that it's more metabolically costly than pregnancy?"

"Seriously?" Max said. She pushed one of the platters of food towards Sasha, who grinned.

"Seriously," Steph confirmed. "Instead of feeding a five-pound baby straight to her gut, you're making enough milk for a ten- or twenty-pound baby. It's exhausting!"

"I don't know how you do it," Max said. "Maybe I'll adopt a four year old. Or eight. How old before they stop trying to eat books?"

Steph and Sasha laughed, but Max's face was serious.

"I mean it. I'd love to be a mom, but I can't run my bookstore *and* take care of a baby."

"That's what employees are for," said Steph.

"I can't afford employees," Max said. "I *love* my store, but business isn't exactly booming. I get by, but I could never hire somebody to work full-time."

"You'd figure it out."

"Though, there's no shame in skipping it," Anna added. She grinned. "Nieces are more fun anyway."

"I'm inclined to agree," Max said. She held out her arms for Gracie, and Sasha relinquished the tiny baby. "Maybe I'll just be the fun aunt."

"Are you implying that I'm not the fun aunt?" Steph said in mock horror.

Max just flashed her a grin.

"You're so young," said Steph. "You don't have to make any decisions just yet."

"She's not that young," Jeff said, swiping a handful of shrimp puffs before they made it from their baking sheet to a serving platter. "Aren't you, like, thirty?"

Max's eyes narrowed. "I'm twenty-nine."

"Same difference," Jeff said. He was the youngest of the five cousins and, even though he was in his twenties now himself, he had taken to teasing Max about her age the past couple of years.

"You're a brat," Max said, and turned her back on him.

Jeff shrugged and stuffed two shrimp puffs in his mouth.

"How are you, Jeff?" Anna asked, steering the conversation away from Max. "Do you like working with Mick?"

Jeff swallowed his food and grinned. "I love it. I never want to do anything else. Besides carpentry, I mean. I'm happy to work with Mick for however long, but I want to start my own business once he retires. Which won't be anytime soon, I don't think. And that's good, because I still have so much to learn. I'm really glad I didn't waste any more time or money on college. Book work is torture for me. I don't mind the math and all, but it drives me crazy doing theoretical stuff. If I'm going to work, I want there to be an end result. I want to *make* something."

"I felt the same way," Sasha said. "It's why I went for interior design instead of some other degree. I love transforming spaces, making something new. I miss it."

"You made a *person*," Jeff said. "It doesn't get more impressive than that."

Sasha smiled at him. "Thanks, Jeff."

The front door opened again, and Todd walked into the kitchen with his girlfriend, Alice. They were an odd couple — Todd in his beige slacks and navy-blue sweater, Alice in a bright red dress with purple leggings — but they were beautiful together.

"We come bearing guests," Todd said. "Three of Ceecee's high school friends are out in the living room."

"I'm on it." Steph picked up a platter of shrimp puffs and walked through to the main room. Todd followed with a bottle of wine and three empty glasses.

"Is there anything I can do to help?" asked Alice.

"I think we're just about ready," Anna said.

Alice drifted over to Max and began to coo at Gracie. Todd's girlfriend was still relatively new in town, but she had grown close to Max and Sasha as her relationship with Todd became more serious. The whole family fell in love with her the year before, when Todd brought her to his mother's house for the family's Thanksgiving feast, and it warmed Anna's heart to see this bond growing between the three young women. None of them had sisters, and she couldn't imagine what that must be like. She was glad that they had each other.

Anna was learning late in life that family was about more than just blood. Pop had loved Anna like she was his own, despite knowing all her life that Anna didn't carry his DNA. She felt the same way about Teddy.

Jeff groaned, and Anna shot him a questioning look.

"Sarah can't be bothered to drive to the park," he muttered, shoving his phone back into the pocket of his jeans. His sister had flown to Maine for the weekend as part of Ceecee's surprise. "She wants me to pick her up from her friend's house on the other side of town."

"*All* the way on the other side of the sprawling metropolis that is Bluebird Bay?" said Max. "However will you manage?"

"It shouldn't take more than an hour or three," Sasha

teased. "Leave now and you might get back before the shrimp puffs are gone."

Jeff stalked out, muttering under his breath, just as Todd walked back into the kitchen with an empty bottle of wine.

"There's another load of guests waiting at the park." He paused to wrap an arm around Alice's shoulders and kiss her temple. "Four of them this time. I'll be right back."

The smile that Alice gave him was effervescent. Anna was delighted by this newest addition to the family; she was already as fond of the girl as she was of Sasha or Ian. She hoped that Alice was here to stay. And judging by the way Alice and Todd looked at each other, that was more than likely.

"How's your great aunt?" Anna asked as Todd walked out.

Alice turned her sparkling smile to Anna. "She's doing so well! Walking without a cane or anything now. Her physical therapist is so impressed."

"And Barnaby?" Sasha asked with a grin. The crotchety old parrot had quickly become a family favorite, and the house that Alice shared with her aunt was lively with frequent visitors.

"He loves the stand that Jeff built for him," Alice replied. "It makes him so happy to climb and play all day. And of course, he was overjoyed to have Auntie home again. He never shrieks at us anymore, and he talks more than ever."

"I'll have to come visit soon," Anna said. "I told a friend of mine about him — she runs a parrot sanctuary down in Mexico — and she sent me the most beautiful wooden toy to hang in his cage."

"How sweet! I can bring it home with me, if you'd like?"

"And let you take all the credit?" Anna exclaimed, and Alice laughed. "No way. I intend to work my way into Barnaby's good graces."

She had tried to pet the huge green macaw on her last visit, and he had responded by trying to take off her pinky finger. But Anna was undeterred. She'd make a friend of him yet.

Half an hour later, all of the guests that they had invited were milling around the living room. Steph's sons had gone off to do their own thing until they were called back for rides, and Sasha was in Steph's bedroom putting Gracie down for a nap. Cee-cee's car pulled up right on time, and Anna shushed everyone as she went to open the door. She walked in, and Steph flicked the lights on as the crowd chorused, "SURPRISE!"

"What's all this?" Cee-cee asked, laughing. "Did I forget my own birthday?"

"It's a wedding shower!" Anna said, hugging her sister and then releasing her. "Obviously."

"I'm too old for a wedding shower."

"You are not!" Anna and Steph said in unison. Cee-cee smiled, blinking back tears. Her friends crowded around her to offer their congratulations, and the next few hours flew by in a mellow haze of laughter and champagne. It was a perfect evening, and Anna was thrilled to see her sister so happy.

Gabe showed up early to take Sasha and Gracie home, and Cee-cee relinquished her sleeping granddaughter. Once her son was safely gone, Anna snatched up her present from the pile and set it in Cee-cee's lap.

"Time for gifts!" Anna crowed. "Mine first!"

Cee-cee's cheeks burned pink as she opened the box and

held up a silky, cream-colored slip that had everyone *oohing* and *aahing*.

"Perfect for the wedding night!" one of Cee-cee's friends exclaimed.

Despite her fierce blush, Cee-cee looked pleased. Most of the other gifts were along the same vein: silk sheets, beeswax candles, and a massage oil that smelled like orange blossoms. Some of her more buttoned-up friends had brought other sorts of gifts, like gift certificates to Bruno's Seafood Restaurant or a personalized cutting board that said *Mick and Cee-cee* at the top.

At the end of the night, after Jeff and Todd had ferried the party guests back to their cars, Anna and Steph helped Cee-cee collect all of her gifts and carry them to her car.

They were just loading the trunk of the car when Ethan drove up, finally home from a long day at work. He looked tired and drawn; Steph must have thought so too, because she hurried over to him and laid a hand on his arm.

"Are you hungry?" she asked. "I can make you a plate. We have plenty of food left over."

"No." Ethan's voice was gruff, but the hand he ran over Steph's back was gentle. "I need a shower. It's been a rough night. Car wreck on the highway. Two people to the hospital and one fatality. It was ugly."

Anna couldn't imagine how awful that job must be sometimes. Her years of wildlife photography had held some brutal moments, but they were always heavily outweighed by beauty and adventure. How could a good man like Ethan endure such an ugly job, day after day?

"I'm sorry to hear that." Steph kissed him on the cheek and stepped aside to let him into the house.

"One good thing, though," Ethan said, pausing in the doorway. "We've got a fresh lead on the Addison murder. I received a photocopied page from Emily's diary from an anonymous source identifying the name of a boy who came into her job a couple times and was watching her, then asked her to a dance just before she went missing. I'll give you one guess at her answer."

Steph squeezed his arm. "I take it she said no."

"Bingo," Ethan replied. His voice was heavy with exhaustion. He kissed Steph's forehead and headed upstairs.

"A man scorned," Anna murmured, turning to look up at the night sky. A dark cloud passed in front of the moon. This many years later, would Emily Addison finally get the justice she deserved?

Anna hoped so.

Because beyond any high notions of justice, the thought of a murderer walking the streets of Bluebird Bay, roaming free amongst her beautiful nieces and the sweet high school girls who passed her house every day on their distance runs, was deeply troubling.

14

MARYANNE

Maryanne busied herself with making a pot of tea while she waited for Alex to arrive. She had seen him nearly every day since they'd met — and the more time she spent with the man, the more she *wanted* to see him. He seemed to feel the same way, because he'd spent basically every evening with her. Sometimes even afternoons.

Mostly they had spent lazy evenings in her cozy cottage, watching movies on her flat screen or just chatting by the fire. One night, he had surprised her with tickets to see a live band, and they went dancing. That was the night they first kissed. The thought still sent a thrill up Maryanne's spine, and since that night, he had come to see her every day. Yesterday he had even helped her cover up the tender plants in her garden; the weather forecast had called for a late frost that hadn't actually manifested.

She hated that they'd met under such awful circumstances, and she hoped that Emily's death wouldn't always loom over them like a dark cloud. Maybe once the case was solved and put to rest, that cloud would dissipate.

But as Maryanne reflected on the past week, she marveled at how much she loved having him around, even in such dark circumstances.

The tea was done and still Maryanne felt fidgety. She glanced at the clock; Alex wasn't due for another ten minutes. Maryanne wandered into her bedroom and decided to start up an essential oil diffuser that a friend had given her for her birthday. She deliberated over the tiny bottles for a moment before choosing lavender. Lord knew her nerves could use it.

Once the scented steam started flowing, Maryanne paused and looked around her bedroom. She loved every inch of this house, loved it far more than any of the mansions she had lived in with her ex-husbands. She had gotten help on the execution from a fabulous interior designer, but the place was every inch her own, from the relaxing bedroom in shades of sage and rose to her icy blue- and espresso-colored vanity.

In some strange way, Alex reminded her of the cottage. Maybe it was just the way that each of them made her feel — comfortable in a way that she had never been in her previous relationships or the oversized houses they'd inhabited.

He was a strong, caring man. None of the flash and style of her former beaus — though he was as attractive as any of them, and more so than most — but there was more to him than that. He was rock steady. Honest. After being cheated on over and over again by weak, flighty men, she deeply appreciated dating someone like Alex. Reliable, comfortable, easy... like her little cottage.

Maybe she was finally growing up — and before the age of sixty! Marianne chuckled at herself and walked back through the house. Alex was due to arrive any moment, and shortly after, they would be joined by the private investigator he had hired, a local named David Shaw. He had agreed to meet them at Maryanne's place to update them on what he had learned so far.

When Alex arrived, there was a level of stress on his face that Maryanne had never seen there before. He looked concerned and downtrodden... more than that, he looked exhausted.

"Sit down," Maryanne told him, running her hand lightly over the muscles of his arm. "I'll bring you a cup of tea."

"Sounds great," Alex said gratefully.

Maryanne joined him a moment later with two steaming mugs of tea. She sat near him on the sofa and asked, "Is something wrong?"

"I just came from Patty's house." Alex wrapped his hands around the hot mug and leaned back. "She was calm at first, sort of out of it... but then she... it was like she snapped back into herself. A rare lucid moment. She started screaming..." He looked at Maryanne with wide eyes. "It was the most heartbreaking sound, Annie. Like she had just heard the news for the first time. Kathleen tried to soothe her, and Patty started throwing things at her. Magazines, a tissue box, nothing much. But she just kept screaming, 'How can I calm down? How can you tell me to calm down when my baby is dead and we don't even know who took her from me?'

"It only lasted a minute or two... but it shook me."

Maryanne blinked back the tears that had sprung to her eyes. She squeezed Alex's knee and he gave her a grateful half smile. Maryanne knew that this would only make him more determined to keep at this until they got to the truth.

Alex took a tentative sip of the tea and gave her another

grateful smile. "This is delicious. I can feel it warming my bones."

It was Maryanne's favorite, a spicy mix of cinnamon and orange peel. She was just about to take a sip when her doorbell rang; she set the mug down on a cork coaster and rose to answer the door. A man and a woman stood on her doorstep. The man must be the private investigator, David Shaw. The woman Maryanne recognized from a local article that had pulled an old photo of her to run alongside a school photo of Emily. There were threads of silver in her dark hair now, though she was younger than Maryanne.

Fallyn Rappaport, the diver who had found Emily's body in a chest on the seafloor. That image still made Maryanne's blood run cold. She introduced herself to the strangers, half conscious of her own words, and invited them in. While they greeted Alex, she slipped into the kitchen to pour two more cups of tea.

"I hope it's alright that I brought Fallyn along," Shaw said as Maryanne returned with the tea. "She's a mastermind when it comes to research, and she's great at getting to the bottom of things."

"Of course," Maryanne said as she handed them their mugs. "It's good of you to help with all this, Fallyn."

"I couldn't not," she said simply. "You knew Emily?"

"Yes." Maryanne sat beside Alex and took a sip of her tea. "I was her babysitter for years, though I wasn't too much older than her. She was like a little sister to me."

"I'm sorry to say that we don't have much yet," Shaw began. All of the air went out of Maryanne's sails. Since the day that Emily's picture appeared in the local paper, Maryanne hadn't had a single night of sleep that didn't feature Emily's face. Emily as a small child. Emily as a preteen. Emily cold and blue, deep underwater. It was wearing on her.

"We've interviewed three of the people from Ricky's list," Shaw continued, "but none of them were very helpful. They were all acquaintance-level friends of Emily's. Not super tight with her, especially towards the time of her disappearance. It seems she had become more and more reclusive in those final months, withdrawing from friends and family... probably spending more time with the older man she was seeing.

"He's our main suspect, of course, but we've yet to get a lead on him. It seems Emily kept their relationship a secret from everyone in her life. If we could just figure out who he was, I suspect we'd have our killer."

"We spoke to one of her high school teachers too," Fallyn added, "and her old boss at the pharmacy. Everyone we've spoken to says that Emily was a good kid. She didn't make trouble. She was pretty quiet... just sort of flew under the radar. We have a couple of people left to talk to, but the chances that they could identify the man Emily was spending time with seem slim."

They continued to talk about potential leads, but Maryanne's thoughts drifted. She had never had a sister, never had a daughter... but some images of Emily were printed as deeply on Maryanne's heart as if she had been her own flesh and blood. She could still see Emily racing her neon-pink bike down a hill, or hanging upside-down from the monkey bars at the park, her golden hair flowing down like liquid sunshine.

It took Maryanne a moment to realize that the room had gone quiet.

"What are you thinking about?" Fallyn asked her gently.

"Sorry." Maryanne flashed the other woman a nervous, apologetic smile. "Just reminiscing about when I used to babysit for her. She was such a sweet kid. So sunny and silly. Shy of new people, but bright and funny once you got to know her."

"You were her babysitter?" Fallyn asked.

"Yes," Maryanne replied. She set her tea down and folded her hands in her lap. "For a couple of years. I just hung out with her on weekends when her mom had work. I was close to both of them, Patty and Emily, until she hit her teens. I was married by then—got married straight out of high school, not one of my better decisions—and we drifted apart some."

Fallyn reached into the pocket of the coat that lay draped over her lap and pulled out a folded piece of paper. She leaned forward and held it out to Maryanne.

"Are any of these names familiar?"

Maryanne took the list of names and looked it over. There were surnames that she recognized, but that was it.

"Nothing that sticks out to me." She handed the list back. "Sorry."

"Can you think of anyone who's not on the list that Emily might have been close to?"

"Like I said, we weren't as close when she was a teenager," Maryanne said reflexively, but then she had a light bulb moment. "Wait," she said, thinking out loud. "Emily had a pen pal from camp. They met when they were... eight, I think?

And they wrote to each other all the time, for years and years. I remember thinking that she was closer to her pen pal than she was to the girls in her class. Emily was always *so* excited when a new letter arrived. They were still in touch when I stopped babysitting, albeit not nearly as often as in the earlier years."

"We didn't find any letters in Emily's room," Fallyn said, "other than the ones from her brother. Do you remember the pen pal's name?"

What *was* that girl's name?

"Renee!" Maryanne blurted as it came to her in a flash. "Renee... something. I'm sorry, I don't remember her last name." She sighed and slumped back. "I'm sorry. It's silly. I just thought... maybe Emily confided in her friend who was far away, who didn't know anyone in town." It seemed like a weak thread, especially since she couldn't even remember the girl's last name.

Fallyn reached over and squeezed Maryanne's hand. "It isn't silly at all."

"We could go back to Patty's house," said Shaw. "See if she remembers Renee's last name, or if there are letters stashed away anywhere. If nothing else, we should be able to find out where Emily went to camp and find out the names of the other kids."

"Patty will be able to tell you," said Alex with confidence. "She remembers a lot about her kids when they were younger. It's just the dark stuff that she blocks out, and everything that's happened since."

"Great." Shaw stood. "If we leave now we should be able to catch her before she goes to bed."

"I have a great gut instinct about this type of thing,"

Fallyn said to Maryanne as she stood, "and my gut is going crazy right now. Thank you. So much."

They walked out, and Alex turned to Maryanne with a grateful smile. "This is the break we've been waiting for."

"I hope so," she said quietly. "I would really love to get some closure. For Patty's sake."

Alex wrapped his strong arms around her, and it was deeply comforting. Maryanne leaned into him, resting her head on his chest. When he pulled back, it was to plant a soft kiss on her lips. She held him closer, surprised that the same man could offer deep comfort and electric chemistry. Both at the same time.

When Alex pulled his face away from hers, Maryanne kept her grip on his arms. "Do you...do you think you'd want to stay tonight?"

He kissed her again and nodded.

"I'd like that."

15

FALLYN

Fallyn sat in the passenger seat of Shaw's car, drinking her... fifth cup of coffee? Sixth? She'd lost count. They had spent the morning chasing dead ends and left just before noon to drive to rural Pennsylvania in search of Dr. Renee Goldberg, Emily's childhood pen pal turned pediatrician.

Patty's caregiver Kathleen had finally gotten a surname for them after two days of prompting. She said that when she did finally get Patty started, it was like a waterfall. Patty spent the rest of the day talking about her kids as if Emily were still nine years old. What any parent in Patty's situation wouldn't give to go back to a time when both of her children were happy and healthy...

Fallyn's stomach burned, and the coffee turned sour in her mouth. She'd had way too much already. She set the paper cup back in the car cup holder and checked the GPS directions. Just another thirty minutes and they'd be there. And not a moment too soon; Dr. Goldberg's business hours were listed as nine to six, and they were due to arrive at

Renee's office at the tail end of her work day. With a bit of luck, they would catch her just before she left.

The gas tank was nearly empty, so they stopped for a hasty fill-up and pee break just before getting to Renee's office at five til six. The front door was unlocked, and a cheerful bell jingled as they pushed it open. It was a nice little doctor's office, soft and welcoming. Nothing like the clinical, gleaming white spaces that housed ten doctors and fifteen physician's assistants.

Light flowed like water across the undersea murals on the walls, playing over the faces of cartoon mermaids. The light was coming from a fish tank on the opposite side of the room. The tank had lights shining from beneath its glass floor and a wide array of tropical fish swimming around within. A colorful poster on the wall next to the tank listed the names of each type of fish next to their pictures.

"Sorry," a voice called out from the back as the door swung shut. "It's just me here. Greta had to head out early today. I'll be right there!"

A tired, kind-faced woman in her fifties came out a moment later, holding a stack of files to her chest.

"Imagine how bad your handwriting has to be for me to rely on my staff to decode it," she said in a warm, self-deprecating voice. "I'm lost without Greta, and she's only been gone a few hours."

She set the folders down on the counter and walked forward, her eyes scanning the space around Fallyn's legs in search of a child. Finding none, she looked between Fallyn and Shaw with a puzzled frown.

"What can I do for you?"

Fallyn spoke in a calm, quiet voice, wary of spooking the woman. "We're here to speak to you about Emily Addison."

Renee straightened, and a wall went up behind her eyes. "Are you the police?"

"No. We're not. My name is Fallyn, and I'm the one who — Well," Fallyn cut herself off with a frown, "are you aware of the recent news regarding Emily?"

Renee looked at her blankly and shook her head.

"You know that she disappeared when she was seventeen?"

Renee nodded. "Her mother sent me a letter not long after, asking if I had seen her."

"Well, I was diving in the Gulf of Maine when I found her... remains," Fallyn explained. "She was right off the coast of Bluebird Bay all these years. Now, she's buried in the cemetery next to her brother."

Renee clapped a hand over her mouth as tears filled her eyes. She took on a faraway look for a long moment, staring off into space, and Fallyn was quiet while Renee processed the news. Finally, the doctor took a long, shuddering breath and turned back to Fallyn and Shaw.

"Okay. Okay. I had a feeling she was gone, but I had hoped..." Renee shook her head.

"This is David Shaw," Fallyn said gently. "He's a private investigator who was hired to find out what happened to Emily. We're hoping to give her mother some closure. Could you spare a few minutes to speak to us?"

"Yes, of course." Renee put her hands over her upper arms, hugging herself like the room had turned suddenly cold.

"We know that you and Emily wrote to each other often, right up through the final months of her life." Renee looked stricken again, and Fallyn paused for a moment before continuing. "We hoped that you might be able to shed some light on those last few months."

Renee looked away and pulled a vape pen from her pocket. She took a long drag, then rolled her eyes apologetically and said, "I know, I know, a doctor vaping, right? Planning to quit soon."

"No judgment here," Shaw rumbled.

Renee took a steadying breath and said, "Yes, we were in contact then. We lost touch for a while in... freshman year of high school, I think it was? Nothing but birthday and Christmas cards for a couple years. But when we were sixteen or so, we started sending letters again. Not weekly like when we were little, but every couple of months." She let out a little laugh that was halfway to a sob. "She was so funny. Like, not in front of a lot of people, but at camp when it was just us, under a sheet with a flashlight? She did the best impressions of the counselors. And she used to send me these comics along with her letters, all of these inside jokes... She was an amazing artist, did you know that?"

"I saw a few of her sketches," Fallyn said.

"We had such a good bond," she reflected sadly. "Real trust. It probably helped that we didn't live close to one another. Who would we share our secrets with anyway, right?"

Fallyn's nerves were buzzing, and she and Shaw exchanged a significant look. Trust was good. It was huge. Maybe Emily told Renee things that she hadn't spoken of to anyone else... like the identity of her creepy, beloved Sugar Bear.

"Did Emily ever write to you about who she was dating?" Shaw asked.

"She wrote about crushes and stuff. We both did. Emily was so shy... I don't think she dated much. She went to school dances with groups of friends, usually, and stood off to the side feeling awkward. Went out with a guy in her class named John a couple times, but it never really went anywhere."

"When was that?" Shaw asked.

Renee thought for a moment. "When she was fifteen? I think that was one of the first letters she wrote after those gap years, because she was so excited to go on her first real date. But by the time her next letter came, it had fizzled out."

"What about closer to her disappearance?" Shaw pressed.

Renee took another drag from her vape pen, eyes going to the fish tank. When she didn't answer, Fallyn pressed, "Do you know if she was dating anyone in her junior year?"

Renee shrugged and shook her head.

"Do you have any of those letters?"

"No," she said immediately. Something about her tone caught Fallyn's attention.

Was the good doctor lying to them?

"I'm sorry I couldn't be more helpful," Renee said. "But it was a long time ago."

"Please call me if you remember anything else... or find any of those letters." Shaw pulled a business card from his pocket and offered it to Renee.

"We'll be in town until noon tomorrow," Fallyn added.

Shaw shot her a look, because they hadn't discussed staying. But Fallyn *knew* that this woman had more to tell them. She conveyed that with a look, and Shaw nodded almost imperceptibly. He walked out, and she hung back to give Renee a long look.

"By all accounts," Fallyn told her quietly, "you were Emily's best friend in the world. The one she told things to that mattered, because she trusted you to take them to the grave. But she's in the grave now, Dr. Goldberg. And more than ever, she needs someone she trusted to come forward and bring her killer to justice. I hope you'll call if you think of anything else at all."

Renee's stricken expression sent a stab of guilt through Fallyn, but she said nothing as she turned on her heel and walked out. She found Shaw waiting by the car.

"What do you think?" he asked.

"I think she really cared about Emily," Fallyn replied, "and that she'll do the right thing. Let's give it tonight and see what happens. We passed a decent-looking motel on the way in. The vacancy sign was on."

Just as Shaw started the car, there was a flash of movement out of the passenger side window and then a tap on the glass. Fallyn turned to see the ashen-faced doctor peering at her in the twilight.

Fallyn rolled down the window, blood buzzing in her ears.

"Barry," Renee said on a huff of breath. "That was her secret boyfriend's name. Barry. He was older than she was, and I don't know his last name. I just know that he lived in Bluebird Bay. Emily thought he was so handsome. I remember she wrote that he had dark brown hair... and a lot of money. If I think of anything else, I'll call." With that, she pushed herself away from the car and scurried back inside.

Fallyn turned to stare at Shaw. "Barry."

"Barry," Shaw repeated with a nod, a grim smile splitting his lips.

They finally had a lead on Sugar Bear.

16

MARYANNE

Maryanne Carpenter Brown stood in front of her closet, utterly flummoxed.

What in the heck did a woman wear to go line dancing? For the most part, downgrading her massive wardrobe to something that would fit comfortably in her cottage had been a relief. But there was the occasional day that she wished she had more to choose from...that one-off outfit tucked in the back corner of her old walk-in closet, absolutely perfect for an odd occasion...and this was one of them.

She ran her hand down the sleeve of a beige cashmere sweater as she thought. She had plenty of swanky party clothes, professional clothes, and even a few pairs of ratty jeans and t-shirts that she wore when she was gardening... but absolutely nothing suited to a night of line dancing.

She let out a sigh as she continued to pick through her lesser-worn clothes, and her mind drifted back to the night that she and Alex had spent together. It had been wonderful, the kind of connection she had all but given up on finding this late in life. She was enjoying his company more and more.

When they were together, they could talk about anything. Not about which couples were on the outs or who had the better vacation homes, like she used to do with her exes. She and Alex talked about things that actually mattered. He loved to hear about her garden — about the medicinal herbs she was learning to grow and even about the things she grew simply because they were beautiful. The way he smiled at her when she doted on her houseplants did something dangerous to Maryanne's heart. And she loved to hear him talk, too. He was so knowledgeable on important topics like health and wellness, and he had so many stories to share about the wide, wild world outside of Bluebird Bay.

Best of all? He didn't sweat the small stuff.

She chuckled as she thought of him picking eggshell out of the omelet she had made him this morning. He hadn't even mentioned it. He had just put it at the edge of his plate without pausing their conversation or his enjoyment of the simple meal. Little things just didn't fuss him, and she thought that was awesome.

He didn't have the sort of wealth she'd chased after in the past — the kind with a mansion and a yacht and a vacation home for each mistress — and Maryanne couldn't care less. To the contrary, she had a hard time understanding why she had ever gone after men with that level of wealth.

Alex wasn't rich, but he was secure. He'd retired from the military and had enough money to spend on what was important to him. Home workout equipment, travel, and his astronomy hobby — not to mention paying a full-time salary to Patty's caretaker and a host of other, smaller monthly charitable donations. Maryanne admired that and was looking forward to their date, even if it might be the type she'd never imagined herself going on.

She pawed through her clothing options one last time, eventually settling on a white jean skirt — that was kind of like jeans, right? — and an off-the-shoulder top with colorful stripes. On a whim, she grabbed a fancy pair of heels the exact shade of the orange stripes on her shirt. She pulled her hair into a loose knot, put on some light makeup, and she was ready to go. At the last moment, she dabbed a citrusy essential oil blend behind her ears in place of perfume. Then, Alex knocked and she hurried to answer the door.

He was wearing blue jeans and a cream-colored button-up shirt, and Maryanne felt happy with her choice of clothes. He was clean-shaven and his hair was freshly cut. They would make a good-looking couple.

"You look handsome," Maryanne told him, picking a piece of lint off of his shirt. The man stood straighter than anyone she had ever met, in a way that made Maryanne remember to keep her own shoulders back and her head held high.

Alex grabbed her hand as she pulled the lint away. He held it to his chest, looking deep into her eyes.

"I really like you, Maryanne. I've been thinking about moving down to Bluebird Bay... getting settled here. I hope that, after all is said and done with Emily's case, I can still have you in my life."

"I'd like that too," Maryanne replied, suddenly misty-eyed.

Alex kissed her, and they stood in the doorway like that for a long moment. Then, he walked her out to his truck and gave her a hand up as she climbed into the passenger's seat. It was a far cry from the low-lying convertibles that she was used to. She felt more like royalty riding up above the world in Alex's truck than she ever had in her exes' expensive leather seats.

"Any news from Shaw or Fallyn?" she asked as he drove through town.

"Not yet," he replied, sounding serious but hopeful. "We should hear something soon, though."

Alex parked near the pier and circled around to help her down out of the truck. They walked hand in hand down the pier, and Maryanne realized that they were headed towards a dive bar at the end. After a lifetime in Bluebird Bay, Maryanne had been in nearly every building in town... but not this one.

Maryanne watched the other people who were going inside. Even the women were dressed in jeans and button-down shirts. Mostly they were wearing cowboy boots. There wasn't another pair of heels in sight. It made her feel silly and vain for putting them on at all.

"I don't think I dressed for this," she said nervously.

"You'll do great," Alex murmured into her ear, placing one hand on the small of her back. "And you look phenomenal."

She smiled up at him, basking in the warm sincerity of the compliment. Then, she threw her shoulders back, lifted her chin, and walked into the bar.

It was warm inside — in more ways than one. The air, the atmosphere, the people smiling in greeting as they walked past. Some of the women were dressed similar to Maryanne, and the lead fiddle player in the band was wearing a sky-blue dress and bright red heels.

They headed straight for the bar, where a woman in plaid handed them each a brown bottle of beer. Maryanne sipped it straight from the bottle, feeling like a kid again.

Alex let a couple of dances pass them by and they stood shoulder to shoulder, drinking their beer and watching the dancers twirl round and round. It looked far too complex for Maryanne to pick up in a single evening, and she was content to stand on the sidelines and watch.

But when the pretty fiddle player struck up another song, Alex pulled the empty beer bottle from Maryanne's hand and set it on the wooden counter with a *thunk*. He took two long strides towards the dance floor, then turned to her with an expectant look.

"Come on," he urged, holding out one broad hand. "This is the perfect song for us."

Maryanne almost refused, but there was something about the look on Alex's face that pulled her forward. She realized that she trusted him. She knew that Alex wouldn't scoff at her efforts or get impatient with her and drop her for another partner. She trusted him to lead her through the steps of a new dance with grace and good humor.

And her trust was not misplaced. Alex had chosen a relatively simple dance, and he grinned with encouragement whether Maryanne was keeping up or fumbling behind.

"You're a natural!" he shouted over the music and laughter, hooking his elbow with hers to spin her round and round. The song was over before she knew it, and she found that she was in no rush to leave the floor. But the next song was twice as fast, and Alex led her back to the bar, his hand strong and gentle around hers.

"That was fun!" Maryanne told him.

"You sound surprised," Alex chuckled. To the bartender, he said, "Can we get some water, please?"

"Maryanne?" the bartender asked. "Is that you?"

She peered at the woman behind the bar, trying to place her. This happened more often than she would like to admit. Bluebird Bay was a small enough town that most people seemed to know who *she* was, but large enough that she often lost track of her acquaintances. This woman was a good ten to twenty years younger than she was, and Maryanne wasn't sure where she knew her from.

"I'm Stella," the bartender told her. She didn't seem offended that Maryanne wasn't able to place her right away. "I work for a catering company part-time, and I tended bar at a few events that you organized."

"Of course! I'm sorry, Stella," she said. "It's good to see you!"

"No worries. It's been years. I *thought* that was you, but I couldn't believe you would come in here. You always struck me as more the champagne and silk type."

Maryanne felt the color rise to her cheeks. "I'm in the garden more than anyplace else these days," she admitted with a smile.

"You were really keeping up out on the dance floor," said Stella approvingly.

"Well," Maryanne shrugged, "I found myself a good teacher."

"I'll say." Stella shot Alex a grin, but his eyes were on Maryanne. "Can I get you anything else?"

"What would you recommend?" Maryanne asked.

"How about a shot of Patron?" There was a good-natured challenge in Stella's eyes.

"Sure." Maryanne's grin widened.

"Two?" Stella asked, looking at Alex.

"Why not," he said. He had told Maryanne that he never drank at home — it was part and parcel with his quest for exquisite good health — but he was always happy to indulge a bit when the occasion called for it. After all, he explained, having fun was the number one way to stay young. What's more, his health was so strong that he seemed as impervious to hangovers as a college kid. She could learn a lot from this man.

They each took a shot of tequila, complete with salt and lime, and then Maryanne pulled Alex back out onto the broad wooden dance floor. Alex gave her the widest grin she had ever seen on his face, and the admiration in his eyes made Maryanne feel like she could do anything. Keeping up was easier than Maryanne had expected, and she laughed with joy as they danced faster and faster. Her hair fell from its bun, swinging loose past her shoulders, and she kicked her heels into a corner, dancing barefoot to keep up with the steps of their final song.

When they left the bar, Maryanne felt better than she had in years. Her hair hung loose, and her shoes dangled carelessly from one hand. Alex held her other hand tight; he pulled her towards him to murmur compliments into her ear. He was constantly telling her how beautiful she was... and what's more, Maryanne was starting to believe him.

They walked together down the pier, her heart soaring above them.

And then she saw something that made her heart drop into the pit of her stomach.

Ex-husband number two walking out of the yacht club, arm in arm with a gorgeous girl less than half his age. Lyle was dressed in a tuxedo, and the girl wore a floor-length gown that glittered with rhinestones. He nearly looked right past Maryanne, then did a double take and took in her disheveled appearance. One side of his mouth curled up in a smirk.

"You're looking...well, Maryanne." Leave it to Lyle to make an insult out of a compliment. Humiliation filled Maryanne's stomach, dripping down to her toes. She dropped her shoes on the ground and slid her feet into them, standing a little higher in her heels.

"Lyle," she said curtly. "This is Alex."

Lyle didn't even glance at the man who stood next to her. He just gave Maryanne another smirk as he ran one hand down his date's back.

"It was good seeing you, Maryanne," he said with feeling. Good seeing how far she had fallen, he meant. Good seeing what she had settled for. Good to show off his latest arm candy.

She just nodded and turned away, smoothing her messy hair away from her face. She walked down the pier, slightly ahead of Alex.

Maryanne felt sick to her stomach. She hated that her cheating asshole of an ex-husband could still make her feel so low and ashamed. Worse than that, he had ruined her night with Alex. She couldn't face him when she felt like this. She hated to let him see how a rich worm like that could tear her down with just a couple of offhand comments. What was *wrong* with her?

"Is everything okay?" Alex asked as he opened the door of the truck for her.

"Yep," she replied. But she couldn't even look him in the eye as she climbed up into the truck and took her seat. The ride back to her place was quiet. Maryanne's stomach churned as she berated herself. Why did she let Lyle do that to her? How did he still have that much power over her?

When Alex parked in front of Maryanne's cottage a short while later, he left the engine running and waited, clearly confused and leaving the ball in her court. Filled with shame, she mumbled her thanks and then ran inside, closing the door behind her.

Damn it.

17

FALLYN

Fallyn and Shaw ended up driving straight back to Bluebird Bay after their meeting with the pen pal turned pediatrician. Shaw dropped her back at the Seal Pup just after midnight, and she stayed up until three in the morning tracking down Emily Addison's elusive Sugar Bear... or trying to.

Bluebird Bay wasn't exactly a big city, but there were *dozens* of results for men named Barry or Barron or Bartholomew... even a Barack. She could narrow things down somewhat by looking at their ages and the years they had spent in Bluebird Bay... but then she had to expand the search to nearby towns.

Add in the fact that Bluebird Bay was a popular tourist town and that the man they were looking for might not even *live* here, might *never* have lived here... and Fallyn could only raise a white flag in defeat. A first name was a start, but it wasn't enough.

She closed her laptop and fell into a fitful sleep.

The next day was no better. Shaw spent the whole day

tracking down one Barry after another to no avail. Fallyn pestered the police department repeatedly, but Detective Jenkins was away from his desk all day.

So far, the lead wasn't panning out.

When she called Shaw at the end of his workday to check in, he sounded dejected and tired.

"I'll keep at it," he assured her, "but to be honest, I've never tried to crack a case this cold. All I do lately is tail middle-aged men to see if they're cheating, or occasionally help worried parents track down their teenagers. It's a lot of credit card trails and sitting in my car all day."

"Is it a dead end?"

"Not quite yet. I have more possibilities to look into. Barrys that lived in other towns along the coastline."

"Have you had dinner?" she asked.

"No dinner, no lunch," he rumbled. "I'm still running on breakfast."

"Running on empty, you mean. Take a break and get something to eat. You'll be sharper in the morning."

"Have *you* eaten?" Shaw asked.

"No," she admitted. "Not yet. I was just about to walk to the diner."

"How about some seafood instead? I'll buy you a top-shelf margarita." When she didn't answer right away, he pressed, "You're doing half the work I'm getting paid for. You should at least get a good meal out of the deal."

"Sure," Fallyn said, half laughing. "That sounds good."

"I'll pick you up in ten," he said, and hung up.

The restaurant was nicer than Fallyn expected, with dark wooden surfaces and a crackling fire at the far end of the dining room. She ordered the shrimp scampi with a glass of white wine, and Shaw ordered a surf and turf plate that would more than make up for his missed lunch. He was quiet as they waited for their food, sipping his margarita and looking out the window. It was dark outside, but she could just make out the white froth of the waves in the moonlight.

"Did Ethan get back to you?" he asked after a while, still looking out at the surf.

"Detective Jenkins?" Fallyn said. "No, I haven't heard from him. I left a message and kept pestering the front desk, but he was out all day."

"Are you done being a reporter?" he asked suddenly, turning to look at her. "Or just done with Chicago?"

"I don't know," Fallyn replied, taken off guard by the change of topic. "Done with crime reporting, for sure. But sometimes I miss being a journalist. The chase, the writing... the deadlines, even. This free-floating existence is still foreign to me, and being a writer is at the core of who I am. I'll go back to writing eventually, once I catch my breath. I don't know yet if that will be articles or something else... a book, maybe. A little bit of everything."

She sighed and looked out to where the water glittered in the moonlight. "I came to Bluebird Bay to escape this kind of thing. To focus on something else. Focus on *myself*. For basically my whole adult life, my whole identity has been Fallyn Rappaport, Investigative Journalist. That's it. I'm not sure who I am without it. But I want to find out."

"Just when I thought I was out," Shaw said, "they pull me back in."

Fallyn laughed. "Yeah, something like that."

"Have you considered that you're really bad at vacations?" he teased gently.

"Just out of practice."

"What made you decide to quit?"

Fallyn took a long sip of her wine. "I hated it," she said at last. "I hated my life. It crept up on me so gradually that it took a long time for me to realize just how much I hated... all of it. My job, my coworkers, my apartment building, that city. But it was all I knew. Even after I realized how unhappy I was there, I kept going. It's what I was good at. It's all I knew.

"Until this one case. My last case. If you can even count it... I didn't turn anything in for that story. Just couldn't write about it. It was too gruesome. The victims were kids, even younger than Emily. I'd seen a lot in my years as a crime journalist, but those little bodies... the things the perp did to them..." Fallyn shook her head. "I just shut down. The idea of writing about it — of *profiting* off of that tragedy — was just abhorrent to me. I took a leave of absence from my job... and just never went back.

"I hid out for months. Basically hibernated all winter. And then I came across this article about a shipwreck, treasure in the Gulf of Maine... and it sparked something in me." She smiled self-consciously, glancing at Shaw to see if he was even listening anymore. He was; she had his full attention. There was something to be said for a man who was quiet because he knew how to *listen*, not because he was completely tuned out.

"I guess it spoke to my inner child, the one I thought had died a long time ago. I had always been fascinated by pirates and ships and treasure. I must have read hundreds of books about that stuff when I was little. Fiction, non-fiction, whatever. So I started reading again, researching. I learned how to scuba dive. And then I came here.

"That gruesome first dive dampened my excitement... but it was wonderful, before I found what I did. It's a whole different world down there — the closest I'll ever come to visiting an alien planet. I would like to get back to it eventually. Even if I don't find anything."

A server arrived with their food: steak and a lobster tail for Shaw, house-made pasta topped with shrimp for Fallyn. They ate in silence for a moment as Fallyn nursed a slight vulnerability hangover. Her pasta was delicious, doused with butter and flavored with a generous amount of garlic. The shrimp were cooked perfectly, marked with delectable lines from the grill.

"What led you to this type of work?" she asked when they were each on their second drink.

"I used to be a cop," he said shortly. Not gruff or irritated, just a man of few words. He set down his knife and fork, looking thoughtful. "I wanted out. The work was too dark, too all-consuming, and it cost me my marriage. Or maybe it wouldn't have worked out anyway, I don't know. But I didn't enjoy the work. Didn't want to take orders from men I didn't respect. So I quit."

"I never even had a marriage to lose," she commiserated as Shaw went back to his food. "I was always too consumed with work."

"I thought I left it all behind, but I was just... adrift. I didn't want to get a corporate job. Didn't want to answer to anyone else. So I ended up here. It's not the greatest job in the world, but at least I'm my own boss. And I was able to set up shop here, to be close to my mother. She's still spry and independent, but she's not getting any younger. I didn't want to be hours away if she needed me."

Fallyn's phone rang then, and she pulled it out of her bag.

"It's the detective," she told Shaw, and answered.

"Hey there Rappaport," he said. "I'm sorry it took me so long to get back to you. I've had a *day*. Anyway, there's nothing I can do with just a first name. That's sixty-three very weak leads and zero time to sort through them. I'm sorry."

"I get it," Fallyn told him.

"I *do* care," he said insistently, as if she had said that he didn't. "I want to help, but the higher ups refuse to greenlight it. I'm meeting with some superiors early next week to try and convince them to authorize me to reopen the case... but we just don't have enough to go on right now. It kills me that we can't do anything for Ms. Addison, but my hands are tied."

"I get it," she said again, looking across the table at Shaw. "Maybe that PI can find something in the meantime." Shaw gave her a grim grin as he chewed his steak.

"Don't do anything rash," the detective warned. "Keep your heads down for now."

"Sure," Fallyn said. "Thanks for getting back to me."

"Of course. I'll call if anything changes."

She hung up and dropped her phone back into her bag. The police department didn't care. How long before Alex gave up and stopped paying Shaw? How long before Shaw quit?

Shaw lifted his margarita to his lips and peered at Fallyn over the salted rim.

"I'm not giving up on this case," he told her.

She shot him a grin, grateful for this steady man who

already seemed to know her well enough to guess what she was thinking. "Neither am I."

Two old men walked past, chatting in their thick Maine accents as they followed their wives out of the restaurant.

"Gutta new grandbaby coming," said one to the other. "Had to go down the cellah to get the cradle."

A sudden realization hit Fallyn like a jolt of electricity.

Forget online databases.

Their best resource right now was the people who had lived in Bluebird Bay for the past fifty years.

She reached out and grabbed Shaw's hand. "We have to talk to Maryanne Carpenter Brown again."

18

CEE-CEE

GABE AND SASHA had finally slipped out of the house for a dinner date, which meant that Cee-cee had Gracie all to herself. She cradled her granddaughter in her arms all evening, even while she slept, marveling over her downy head and perfect little fingers. The baby was so sweet that Cee-cee just had to create a cupcake in her honor. She would call it the Amazing Grace. She could use malted milk in the batter as a nod to that wonderful brand-new human smell, maybe a malted milk chocolate, and then she would make pink frosting the exact shade of Gracie's little pink bow of a mouth. Raspberry, maybe. Or strawberry.

There was a knock on the front door, but before Cee-cee could even get up from the recliner, Max opened the door and walked in carrying a bag of Thai food. Cee-cee laughed in surprise.

"What are you doing here?"

"What? You thought I would let you hog all the baby snuggles for yourself?" Max grinned and set the bag of food down on the dining table. "Ian had to work late and I thought I'd stop by for some quality time. Relinquish the baby."

Max walked across the room with her hands outstretched, and Cee-cee handed Gracie over. She went into the kitchen for dishes and served up the food that Max had brought. She gave Max most of the pad thai — her favorite since childhood — and served herself a bowl of green curry over white rice. It was studded with pieces of white fish, bamboo, and baby corn — and it smelled divine.

Max cuddled the sleeping baby for a few minutes before setting her down in her bassinet and joining Cee-cee at the table. With no baby of her own, she hadn't mastered the art of eating one-handed. Cee-cee wondered idly if Max would ever become a mother. Her daughter would make a wonderful mother, Cee-cee knew, but Max rarely expressed interest in motherhood. Maybe she would be the fun aunt of her generation, like Anna had been to her.

"How are things at the bookshop?" Cee-cee asked. That's where all of Max's energy went these days. She had always been focused on her career, but it wasn't until opening her own bookstore that Cee-cee had seen her daughter come alive with joy.

"It's been a fun week," Max replied between bites of orange rice noodles. "You know that slam poetry night I started a while back? It was just a desperate attempt to get people into the shop. I didn't expect to actually *like* it."

"And you do?" Cee-cee asked. She ate a bite of rice with curry sauce, marveling at the sweet and savory decadence. It packed a punch, too. She went to the kitchen in search of something to drink.

"I *love* it. There are some brilliant poets in this town, Mom. It's better than a night at the movies. Even Ian thinks so. And even when the poems aren't that good, there's something beautiful about a person getting up there and pouring their heart out in public, you know? They're so brave."

Cee-cee returned to the table with two bottles of ginger ale. "I love that you're giving people a space for that."

"It's really picking up steam. People are starting to come in from out of town. It was *packed* this week. I probably violated a few fire codes. But it was a blast. There's a whole community being built up around it. And it's been a great way to network with local poets and artists. One of my favorites is coming in this weekend to do a reading and a book signing."

"I love that. And Ian's business is still booming?"

"Yeah! He and Jeff are working on a sixth room now. Actually, it's the basement, this really big space that Ian's been saving. It's going to be an ancient Egypt theme, like an underground tomb. He wants every room in the building up and running by summertime. He's planning to hire a full-time employee for summer too, so he doesn't have to work such crazy hours."

"What about you? Any help on the horizon?"

"I'm not there yet. There are some months that I look back at the books and realize that I could have afforded full-time help, but then there are other months that I barely scrape by. It would just kill me to hire someone and then have to fire them because we had a few slow months. So for now, I'm just setting aside money from the good months, creating more of a cushion."

"That's so wise," Cee-cee said, nearly bursting with pride.

Max shrugged self-consciously and changed the topic, sounding hesitant now. "I'm going out to dinner with Dad later this week for his birthday. He invited Gabe too, but Gabe wouldn't commit."

Cee-cee thought back to how harried Nate had looked when she had run into him.

"How's he doing?" she asked gently.

"Honestly? I think he's a little butt-hurt about you getting remarried, but he's a grown man. He'll be okay."

"I know that."

"Do you?" Max raised one eyebrow and pointed her fork at Cee-cee. "You're always worrying over him like he's some idiot kid. I know he's made some stupid choices, but he's a grown-ass man. And he's not your responsibility."

Cee-cee raised her eyebrows. "You're right."

"Sorry." Max grinned apologetically and picked up another forkful of pad thai. "I just don't want him to spoil your happiness. He did that for so many years, and your life is just so *good* now."

"If he did, it's because I let him," Cee-cee said quietly. "One last question, and then I'm done."

Max rolled her eyes, mouth full of noodles.

"Is he paying back the money that Ian loaned him?"

Max swallowed her food and said in an exasperated voice, "Yes, Mother. Right on schedule."

"Good. That's all I need to know."

"I don't even want to go out to dinner with him," Max muttered, squeezing more lime over her pad thai. "I just felt bad saying no when it's his birthday."

It hurt Cee-cee's heart that her children's relationship with their father was so fractured. She had done everything she could over the years to give them quality family time together, but he had just never put in enough time. He had tried when they were small, but every year work had taken over more and more of his life. By the time their children were entering their adolescent years, it had drained all the fun out of him; even when he was with them, he could be so critical and cold.

It wasn't that she worried about Nate for his own sake. At least, not much. She worried that he would disturb her children's peace of mind. But ironically, she was doing that with her worrying. She smiled at herself and shook her head as she took a bite of tender white fish.

Max was right. It was time to put Nate behind her. Hopefully his weirdness would fade after she had been married for a few months, and they could coexist peacefully at events like Gracie's first birthday and Max's someday wedding.

Gracie woke and started to fuss. Max scooped her up and tried without success to calm her, but the baby continued to mewl in a way that was just short of a wail. Cee-cee hurried to grab a bag of milk from the fridge and warm it up in one of the little glass bottles that Sasha had left for her.

"She absolutely refuses to take a bottle," the young mother had worried earlier that day.

"Well of course she's not going to take one from you when she has the real thing right there," Cee-cee laughed. "You go and enjoy yourselves. I promise I won't let your baby starve. If she needs you, I'll send an SOS. Okay?"

Sasha had smiled shyly and agreed. She was always wary

of accepting help, but Cee-cee knew how excited she was to go out to dinner with Gabe and see Alice's band play live at a local bar.

Cee-cee tested the milk on the inside of her wrist, then took her squalling granddaughter back from her Auntie Max and offered her a bottle. Gracie took it immediately and stared at her with wide eyes, surprised to be getting sustenance from anyone but her mother and not entirely sure of the rubber nipple in her mouth. Then, she relaxed into her grandmother's arms, content with the warm nourishment that was filling her tiny stomach.

"Ian just texted," Max whispered, as if the baby was sleeping rather than eating. "He's done for the night. I'm going to head home."

Cee-cee kissed her daughter on the cheek. "Thanks for dinner."

"Anytime," Max said, still whispering. "Bye, Gracie."

She slipped out the door, closing it gently behind her, and Cee-cee settled down on the couch. Gracie was alert and active for a little while after her meal, flinging her arms and legs around as if she wanted to swim off through the air. Then, she settled back to sleep in Cee-cee's loving arms.

Cee-cee sent Gabe and Sasha a quick text encouraging them to stay out as late as they liked, telling them that the baby was fed and asleep. She was set to meet up with her sisters at the diner, but she didn't mind showing up a little late. Generally speaking, she was a punctual person... but there was nowhere she would rather be than here with her Amazing Grace.

When Gabe and Sasha finally got home, Cee-cee was asleep on the couch with Gracie on her chest. Sasha whisked the baby off to feed her, and Cee-cee smiled up at Gabe. Her son looked more relaxed and content than he had in a long time.

"Good night out?" she asked.

"The best. Thanks, Mom."

"Anytime, sweetie." Cee-cee stood and stretched. The clock on the wall told her that she was already late to meet her sisters at the diner. Maryanne Carpenter Brown had called and asked them to meet her tonight. Apparently, the amateur sleuths who were trying to crack the Addison case thought that the Sullivan sisters might be able to help. Cee-cee was dubious that they had anything to offer that might aid the detectives, but of course she was willing to try. Her heart broke all over again for Patty Addison every time she thought of what had happened to Emily. Anna had sounded excited to be a part of the investigation; Cee-cee would much prefer to go straight home to her fiancé. But a promise was a promise. And she could go for a slice of Eva's blueberry pie.

"Hey Gabe," she asked on her way out, "have you seen your dad lately?"

Immediately, Gabe's face closed in on itself. "A few weeks ago. He's come to visit *once* since Gracie was born. You'd think he'd show some interest in his first grandbaby, but... not so much."

"He always did have his own priorities," Cee-cee murmured. "I wonder—"

"Don't," Gabe interrupted.

She blinked at him in surprise. "Don't what?"

"Don't worry about him. Or us, for that matter. You're happy, remember? You're about to get married! Stop trying to make the happiness of others your responsibility."

"You know," she said with a smile, "Max told me more or less the same thing."

"Well, in spite of that, it's very good advice."

"Yes, my children are very wise."

"One of us, anyway. Max gets lucky here and there. But me, I've got wisdom dripping out my ears." Gabe pulled her in for a hug, and she marveled for the umpteenth time at how tall and strong her boy had become. "Thank you for babysitting, Mom. We really appreciate it."

"Anytime," she told him again. There was nowhere she would rather be. She was even tempted to offer to sleep over, to take Gracie for the night and let them get some solid sleep. But there would be countless opportunities for sleepovers with her grandbaby. She was so excited for the day that Gracie was old enough to sleep over at her place.

Tonight, though, there was an investigative reporter waiting to speak with her... and a slice of blueberry pie with her name on it.

19

FALLYN

MARYANNE BROWN HADN'T KNOWN who the mysterious Barry was — but Fallyn had to admit that the woman had really come through when they had called and asked her if she could pull together a sampling of people who had lived in Bluebird Bay all their lives. In less than twenty-four hours, she'd not only gotten a list of names, she'd also put together a meeting at the diner right down the road from the Seal Pup Inn.

The cool evening air soothed Fallyn's nerves. She was feeling hopeful, ready to see what the old school Bluebird Bay townies might know.

She walked into Mo's Diner, pushing past the *closed* sign to find most of the group already assembled. Maryanne was seated at the diner's largest table with two men and a woman, all around her age. Eva, the omnipresent waitress, was bringing everyone coffee as a curly-haired woman urged her to sit down and rest a while.

When Fallyn had spoken to Maryanne on the phone and asked her to get together a small group of people who had lived in Bluebird Bay around the time of Emily's disappearance, Maryanne had agreed instantly and had quickly gotten together a short list. She had sounded excited to be of help. But as Fallyn looked at her now, Maryanne seemed off. Her face looked pale, which may have been just a lack of the intricate makeup she usually wore... but she looked sad too.

Then again, maybe meeting old acquaintances at night to discuss the murder of a girl she had loved like a sister wasn't Maryanne's idea of a good time.

Fallyn felt excited to be chasing down such a promising lead, but for everyone else it must be a sobering situation. She tried to get her face in order as she walked towards the table. Somber without being intimidating...

"Hello," Maryanne greeted her, giving her a smile that looked strained but sincere.

"Hi, Maryanne," Fallyn said. "Thank you for arranging this."

"Of course," Maryanne replied. "This is Anna, and her... fiancé? No? Sorry. Her person, Beckett."

Anna gave Maryanne an exasperated look, then reached out to shake Fallyn's hand.

"And this is Mick," Maryanne continued, "another Bluebird Bay native. Oh, and that's Steph," she added as another woman walked in.

"Is it okay for you to be here?" Anna asked after Steph shook Fallyn's hand. "I thought Ethan didn't want them to keep pursuing this."

"I know what it's like to love someone and have no idea what happened to them," Steph said quietly. "I want to help, if I can. I'll ask forgiveness instead of permission on this one if

I have to... but I don't think he'd mind. He's been chasing his tail since day one on this case, trying to get his supervisors to let him pursue it... but no one seems to care."

"I care," Shaw said from the door. He looked to Fallyn. "Sorry I'm late. I had someone barge into my office at closing time, demanding that I tail her husband *tonight*, and it took a while to get out of there."

Fallyn smiled at him and turned back to the group, taking a seat at their table. "Thank you for coming, everyone. I can't tell you how much I appreciate it."

"The Sullivan sisters grew up in Bluebird Bay," Maryanne told her, gesturing to Anna and Steph, "and Eva has lived here for... what, forty years?" she asked the waitress.

"Oh, something like that." Eva set two cups of coffee down in front of Fallyn and Shaw, then joined them at the table with a mug of her own.

"Anna and Steph are Gabe's aunts," Maryanne added.

Fallyn looked at the women in surprise. Small town.

"He's a wonderful young man," she told them. "He was so kind to me from the get go, and so steady after the shock I got down there... he was such a calming presence."

"He was always a good kid," Steph said.

"I don't know how much Maryanne told you," Shaw said, impatient with the pleasantries, "but thanks to her we were able to track down an old camp friend of Emily's. She told us that Emily wrote to her about an older man she was seeing named Barry. That's all we've got. A preliminary search hasn't turned up anything promising, so we're hoping that one of you might be able to help us out. He was older than Emily and frequented the pharmacy where she worked."

"We knew a Barry in school," Anna said. "Didn't we?"

"I don't remember any Barrys," Steph replied.

"He was a couple years younger than me... maybe you wouldn't have known him. I didn't know him all that well, I just remember that he existed."

"But he would have been close to Emily's age," Maryanne protested. "She wrote that Barry was an older man."

"A few years is a big difference at that age," Anna said. "If she was seventeen and he was in his twenties, that's enough for a high schooler to think of him as an 'older man'."

"Are you talking about Seamus Barron?" Mick asked.

"Maybe?"

"That's my friend Jack's little brother. I seem to remember his friends calling him Barry sometimes. But he went to college in California and never moved home. He wasn't here then."

"Not even visiting?"

"He wouldn't do a thing like that," Mick said firmly. "He was a good kid."

"I can look into it," Shaw said, "make sure he wasn't in town then. But it sounds unlikely. Does anyone else have an idea?"

"There was a trucker who came through that summer, before Emily went missing," Eva mused, looking off into space. "I'm not sure I recall his name. It *could* have been Barry."

"I don't think summer fits the timeline," Anna told her gently.

"The Peterson family has a Barry, don't they?" Steph said.

"He's too young," Mick replied. "He would've been a kid when it happened."

"Burt!" Eva exclaimed, slapping the table with one hand. "It wasn't Barry. The trucker's name was Burt!" She smiled sheepishly. "Sorry. Senior moment."

Fallyn leaned back in her chair and sipped her coffee black, feeling their lead slip away. How could a man go unnoticed for years in a town this small? Did he live in another town nearby? Was he a college kid at the time? Anna was right when she said that a teenage girl might refer to a boy in his twenties as an 'older man'. But was there even a college around here?

She was just turning to Shaw to ask if he had checked the local college rosters when the door to the diner opened again. Another woman walked in, smiling apologetically at the group gathered around the table. She bore such a strong resemblance to both Steph and Gabe that Fallyn knew at once she must be Gabe's mother. Mick rose from the table to embrace her.

"That's Cee-cee," Maryanne muttered, sounding thoroughly down now. Maybe she was losing hope too. As Cee-cee joined them at the table, Maryanne introduced Fallyn and Shaw.

"I'm sorry for coming so late," Cee-cee said. She paused to smile at Eva and thank her for the cup of coffee she'd handed her. "I was on grandma duty. What did I miss?"

"Not much," muttered Maryanne.

Anna asked her sister, "Do you remember anyone named Barry who lived in Bluebird Bay when we were younger?"

"Sure," Cee-cee said. "Chaz Bartholomew. He was a year

ahead of me in high school. The football team used to call him Barry for short...I think he actually still lives in town."

She paused as everyone stared at her, gobsmacked that she had come up with a name that fast.

"Did I do good?" she asked, half-laughing. Then, she paled. "Wait. Are you saying that Barry may have had something to do with Emily's murder?"

"We have no idea," Fallyn said, pulling a pen and notepad from her bag, "but we are definitely going to want to speak to him."

She glanced at Shaw, whose eyes were bright with interest, and turned back to Cee-cee. "So, what else can you tell us about Chaz Bartholomew?"

20

MARYANNE

When Maryanne plugged Anna Sullivan's address into her car's GPS system, she was surprised to realize that her house was close enough to ride her bike to. Not in *these* shoes, she amended as she pulled out of the driveway, but still.

Close enough.

Just a couple of years ago, she would have listed Anna as one of the people she despised most in the world. Seemingly flaunting her good looks and her exciting world travels, always making Maryanne feel "less than".

Now, of course, she realized that Anna certainly wasn't trying to make her feel bad. She was just living her life, unapologetically...

Sort of like you're supposed to be doing, a little voice in her head whispered.

But dang, did old habits die hard sometimes.

With Anna, though, she was completely over those old resentments.

After they wound up at the same cancer support group, she realized that her dislike of Anna was born of jealousy over the fact that her first husband had the hots for Anna since they were in high school... and he never let Maryanne forget it. Maybe in those early years, she had been sure that Anna was doing something to encourage him, lead him on... now, she realized that he was just a miserable human being who had used those sideways remarks as a way to keep Maryanne in her place.

Under his thumb.

It was so strange how trauma and fear sometimes brought such clarity. Despite the awfulness of it all, the cancer had been a gift in more ways than one. Her fear had thrown everything into such stark relief and made Maryanne realize that without her health, she had nothing.

Her new passion for self-care was nothing like the myopic, damaging dieting of her youth. This was all about nourishing her body and soul. She started eating well, really *feeding* herself, enjoying her food without counting calories. She found that she loved to spend long afternoons gardening in the sunshine far more than she loved schmoozing with the rich and richer. And for the first time in her life, she truly loved her body.

When she thought of all the years that she had wasted worrying about cellulite and starving herself to fit into a certain dress size, Maryanne felt such grief and compassion for the miserable young woman she had been.

And when she thought of the way that she had behaved to Anna for most of their lives, she felt such shame.

But she had apologized, and Anna had been big enough to wholeheartedly accept her apology. Ever since, they'd been friendly. They stopped to chat when they ran into each other around town. This, however, would be new territory for them. A one-on-one meal, just the two of them, face to face. When Anna had invited her the night before, as they'd all filed out of the diner, Maryanne had nearly said no. She just hadn't been feeling herself since that awkward end to her date with Alex.

She knew that she should call him — she'd walked away so abruptly that night — but she had no idea of what she could say to put things right. She didn't know how to explain why she had suddenly shut down. She didn't want him to see how weak she was. What if it made him think that she was still hung up on her ex?

Maryanne let out a groan. She couldn't think about that right now. Getting through brunch with Anna Sullivan without making a fool of herself would take all the emotional energy that she had. She pulled up in front of a beautiful craftsman-style house and put her car in park.

There was a ceramic dish of baked oatmeal resting on the floor of the passenger's side, and Maryanne picked it up. Still warm from the oven, it was her contribution to today's meal. A homey peace offering. Was she still trying to convince Anna that she didn't have her nose up in the air?

Here, I've brought this simple peasant fare for us to enjoy. See, I cook, just like a normal person.

Maryanne chuckled. There, at least she could laugh at herself. There was hope for her yet.

She headed up the walkway, and Anna greeted her at the door with a wide smile.

"Hi Maryanne! I'm so glad you could make it. Beckett got a call from someone who needed a tow, so it's just you and me."

Walking into the beautiful wooden living room, what

stood out to Maryanne were the photos on the walls. They were worthy of National Geographic covers. Then again, she reminded herself as she admired one of a polar bear on the ice, some of them probably *had* been on the cover of National Geographic — or at least featured inside. She knew that Anna was talented and successful... but these pictures were something else. One in the hallway of some sort of wildcat was particularly beautiful; it stared straight into the camera, golden eyes bright in the sunlight.

Anna waited patiently while Maryanne admired her work. She didn't brag or preen. When Maryanne asked where photos were taken, she offered funny, self-deprecating stories. Apparently, she had broken a bone getting the one of the white fox.

"And you still have it up on your wall?" Maryanne laughed.

"Maybe I'm still trying to convince myself it was worth it," Anna said wryly. "Not that it was. My leg still aches when there's a frost coming."

"That's a superpower I wouldn't mind having," said Maryanne. "I'm never sure when to cover my rose bushes and other tender plants, so I'm always taking the covers on and off. Same with my transplants in the spring."

"I'll be sure to tell you if we have a late frost coming," Anna said with a grin. She led Maryanne into the kitchen, where the table was set with a fantastic array of brunch treats.

"Did you make all this?" Maryanne gasped.

Anna laughed. "Nothing but the coffee. I ran out and picked the food up from that new bakery on Main. I'd just finished setting it out when you pulled up. Come and eat before the lox gets cold."

"Isn't lox supposed to be cold?" Maryanne said with some hesitation, and Anna laughed again.

"It's all cold. That was me making fun of myself for not making a hot breakfast."

"No, it looks amazing. And I brought something warm." Maryanne set her baked oatmeal on the table and pulled off the lid. It was studded with pecans and cranberries, sweetened with maple syrup.

"That smells delicious." Anna poured two big cups of coffee and sat down at the table.

Maryanne joined her and helped herself to a fat slice of sourdough with bright green pesto cream cheese and smoky orange lox. As they chatted about Maryanne's garden and their favorite places to eat in Bluebird Bay, she marveled at how easy Anna was to talk to.

She wished that she hadn't wasted so many years hating Anna Sullivan for something that had nothing to do with her. Maryanne had more acquaintances than she could count, but she only had one really close friend — and Heather kept busy.

She realized now that she needed more women in her life. This noncompetitive feminine energy was so healing, nothing like the draining effort of socializing with trophy wives or dating one man after another. She had missed out on that balance for too long, always competing with other women, never really letting them in.

There was a lull in the conversation as Maryanne loaded her plate with fruit salad and Anna poured each of them a fresh cup of coffee. Then, Anna said, "I really hope that our meeting yesterday helps that couple that's working to find answers about Emily. Though it would be chilling if that Chaz guy was the one. I know his face; he was a friend of Cee-cee's ex-husband, and I still see him around town now and again. The thought that he could do something like that... that *anyone* in Bluebird Bay could do something like that..." Anna trailed off and shook her head.

"I know what you mean," Maryanne murmured. Her stomach had dropped at Cee-cee's answer, because she *knew* that guy. He ran in the same circles as her second ex-husband. She hadn't made the connection herself because she only knew him as Chaz. The thought that she had chatted and sipped champagne with Emily's killer made her want to vomit. She poked listlessly at the fruit salad, her appetite deserting her.

"Fallyn told me that she and the PI would devote the whole day to researching the guy to find out his whereabouts during that time period," she told Anna. "They're going to find out whether or not he had a boat... or access to a boat."

"I hope that Cee-cee's lead will give them enough for the police to reopen the case."

"Me too," said Maryanne.

"What was she like?" Anna asked.

"She was the sweetest kid." Maryanne met Anna's gaze and smiled. "I couldn't believe my luck, getting *paid* to hang out with her every week. It was like getting the kid sister I had begged my mom to give me for years, but I still walked away with pocket money." She looked out the window, remembering. "I felt bad, sometimes, taking it from Patty... one week, when they were strapped for cash, I just snuck my wages into the pocket of Patty's coat on my way out the door.

She would never let me work for free. It's so unfair, Anna. All of it. She did everything for her kids. Only to have both of them stolen from her. It's just not right."

There was a long pause, and when Maryanne looked up, Anna was watching her with an intensity that caught her off guard. When she met her eyes, Anna said, "I invited you over today because I wanted to check in. One on one. I can only imagine how stressful the news about Emily must have been, but you just looked so worn out last night... I just wanted to make sure there wasn't anything else going on."

Maryanne's first thought was of her fumbled date with Alex, but there was such concern in Anna's eyes. It reminded her of the way people had looked at her when she told them about her cancer diagnosis. And then, with a sudden flash of clarity, she realized that *that's* what Anna was worried about. She thought that Maryanne's cancer was back.

Maryanne smiled, touched to the core by Anna's concern. "I'm fine, Anna. I'm healthy. My heart just goes to pieces every time I think of Emily, and I have to duct tape it back together again after each visit with Patty... but I'm good. My life is good. My health is better than it's ever been. And..." she paused, then took the plunge, "I met someone."

Anna had relaxed when Maryanne assured her of her good health, and now she grinned. Leaning back with her coffee mug held in both hands, she said, "Tell me everything."

Maryanne chuckled and ate a piece of mango, wondering how to describe Alex Orloff. Anna waited impatiently, eyebrows raised above the steam from her coffee.

"He's different from any of my ex-husbands," she began.

Anna interrupted with a snort of laughter and said, "Thank God for that!"

Maryanne felt the briefest flicker of irritation... and then she laughed too. "No kidding," she said with a wry grin. But the grin slipped away when she thought of Lyle. "We ran into one of them the other night. The second one. And the moment I saw him... I don't know, Anna. It's like I went into this shame spiral. First, I felt ashamed because he was coming out of a freaking Carnation Ball in a tux or whatever, while I had just left a hoe down and looked like a sweaty mess in denim. And the next second, I felt ashamed for feeling ashamed about that at all, you know? That one was harder to shake... and I let it ruin my night with Alex. That's his name," she explained belatedly. "Alex. He lives a little ways away, but he came to check on Patty. The man's been taking care of her for twenty-five years like she was his own mother, just because he was good friends with her son and there was no one else to look after her."

"That's a rare kind of man," Anna said.

"Don't I know it." Maryanne sighed and leaned back in her chair. "What's more, I think he stuck around for *me*. He pays someone to look after Patty full-time, and it's not like he had to stick around to talk to the PI he hired in person. But he stuck around, even moved from the motel he was staying in to this nice Airbnb by the beach. Walking distance from my house..."

"This Alex guy is *into* you!"

"He told me as much," Maryanne admitted, looking down into the dregs of her second cup of coffee. Despite the caffeine, she felt low and tired. "He had just told me that night how much he liked me. Said that he wanted to move here. But then I let my ex get into my head, and I rushed off with barely a goodbye. Lord only knows what he thinks of me now, seeing the type of asshole I used to be attracted to. I botched it. I always botch it. Remember Reggie?"

"That's the last guy you dated, yeah? He seemed nice."

"He *was* nice," Maryanne said. "He's a really good guy. And he liked me. I just... I guess I couldn't trust that he was *actually* as nice as he seemed. And so I kept poking at him, getting under his skin. I didn't even realize it at the time, what I was doing. I just kept saying things, all these little barbs, being mean for no reason. And finally he got sick of me. Didn't blow up or say ugly things like I expected. Just told me that he didn't think we were compatible."

"Have you talked to Alex since that night?" Anna asked.

Maryanne shook her head. "He called yesterday... didn't leave a message. And I didn't have the guts to call him back. I don't even know what to say."

"Try being honest with him," Anna said gently. "Tell him what you just told me."

Maryanne winced. "That sounds terrifying."

"Being vulnerable can feel scary... but it's the only way to build something real."

"I've spent so many years putting up these walls between me and... well, everyone. But especially the men I've dated. Probably because I *needed* those walls with most of those scumballs, to keep myself safe. But I don't want to do that with Alex. I just don't know how *not* to."

"You start with honesty," Anna said. "You've made so many huge changes in your life, Maryanne. You sold that fancy house and started really taking care of yourself. You realized what's important. That's the main gift of a cancer scare, I think. It made *me* realize how important my family was to me. Looking death in the face can give us a lot of clarity."

Maryanne smiled at her, feeling closer to her old nemesis than ever. "I've thought the same thing."

"I think Alex came into your life at the perfect time. If I were you, I'd high tail it over to his place and tell him exactly how you feel."

Maryanne set her empty mug down with a *thunk*. "You're right. I'll do it." She paused and looked over the table, which still held enough food to feed a large family. "Just as soon as I help you clean up."

"No way," Anna said. "Get out of here before you lose your nerve. I didn't cook a thing — thank goodness — so the least I can do is the dishes. Anyway, I'm going to leave it all out until Beckett gets back. I'll give you your dish back next time I see you."

Maryanne smiled, grateful for this new friendship. Grateful that Anna assumed there would be a next time. "Okay. I'll do it."

"Atta girl."

Maryanne stood and turned to go. Then, she turned back to Anna. "I'm going dancing with Heather next week. There's this live band we love that plays old hits. Would you like to come? You're welcome to bring your sisters along."

Anna grinned and nodded. "That actually sounds really fun."

Maryanne walked out the door with a new spring in her step. She had friends, plural. That gave her the courage that she needed to face Alex. There were butterflies in her stomach, but they were the good kind. Mostly.

She almost chickened out on the way there; she even

parked in front of her house. But instead of going inside, she walked the two blocks over to the cottage that Alex had rented when he decided to extend his stay in Bluebird Bay. And then she stood on his doorstep, paralyzed by fear, and considered turning right back around.

Alex opened the door and regarded her with a bemused grin. "Were you going to knock?"

"I was summoning up the courage."

Apprehension flickered across his face. "For what?"

"To apologize," she blurted. "I'm so sorry, Alex. I had so much fun with you the other night. And I want to keep trying new things with you, I do. I just... I've never felt this connected to anyone before. I guess I got spooked. And I'm sorry for avoiding you. It just took me a minute to process everything I was feeling. Did I blow it?"

Alex looked at her for a long moment, and she couldn't read what was going on behind his stoic expression. Then, his mouth curled up in a soft smile. "I was just about to go whale watching. Care to join me?"

Maryanne's anxiety melted away as she returned his smile. "I do. I definitely do."

21

FALLYN

When the words on the screen began to blur together into an incomprehensible mess, Fallyn closed her laptop with a groan. She had spent most of the day in Shaw's office, only leaving to pick up their meals while Shaw carried on working. They had even slept there the night before — if you could call it that. Shaw had dozed in his office chair for an hour or two while Fallyn napped on a small and deceivingly uncomfortable couch. The undersized sofa had done something unfortunate to her spine; she felt like she'd slept on a pile of elbows.

Fallyn set her laptop aside and stood, back cracking in a way that was equally cathartic and concerning. Then, the door opened, and Shaw returned from a food run carrying two large cups of coffee and a pastry bag. Fallyn grabbed a cup from the cardboard holder the moment he stepped through the door.

"Bless you," she murmured as she took her first sip.

He tossed the paper bag from the bakery onto his desk and sank into his chair to take a long drink of his own coffee.

Even exhausted, the man was handsome. His face still showed the strong lines that most men his age had lost to paunchiness.

Fallyn blinked and looked away. She reached into the pastry bag and pulled out a bear claw.

"Dinner fit for a queen," she said. Shaw raised one eyebrow ironically, but she meant it. Fallyn took a bite, savoring the flakey croissant and flavorful marzipan. It was heavenly.

"What do you think?" she asked as he bit into a muffin. "Have we got enough to convince Ethan's bosses to have a talk with Chaz Bartholomew?"

Shaw frowned and took another sip of coffee. Then, he shook his head slowly.

"You know we don't." His voice was heavy with regret and frustration.

Despite twenty-four hours of digging, they didn't have much. They'd gone to the library that morning and pored over countless articles about Emily's disappearance, searching for any mention of Chaz Bartholomew. Aside from some high school football accolades years before Emily's disappearance, a wedding announcement, and a brief mention of some bench that he and his wife had donated to a local park in his mother's name after her death... there wasn't much. He and his wife, Nancy, appeared every few years in photos from charity auctions and other such events. He was mentioned in a recent article about his son's extravagant wedding. All boring stuff. Certainly nothing linking him to Emily's murder.

Chaz and his wife owned a house on the outskirts of town, but he had never owned a boat.

At least, no boats had ever been registered under his name. Even using all of Shaw's fancy software, there was no indication that the man had ever committed a crime.

By all accounts, he was a model citizen.

His record was so squeaky clean that it made Fallyn wonder. What kind of kid made it through to adulthood without so much as a speeding ticket? Certainly not one who'd received a convertible the day he turned sixteen. Chaz came from old money. Did his family have ways of wiping the slate clean? Brushing things under the rug?

But feelings weren't facts. The truth was, the cops wouldn't touch this thing with a ten-foot pole. And yet... something in Fallyn's gut told her that they should.

"He was already married when Emily disappeared," she said. Was she trying to talk herself out of going with her gut? That was never a good idea. And yet, she kept talking, thinking out loud, her brain fried from lack of sleep. "They've been married all this time... and they look happy on social media."

Shaw snorted. "Who doesn't?"

"I'm not saying it lets him off the hook, but it raises some questions... Why wouldn't Emily mention in her diary that he was married? It's a small town — she had to know."

"She didn't even mention his *name* in her diary," said Shaw. "She must have been worried her mother would find it. Anyway, it was before social media. He could have kept it a secret."

"But surely a new wife would have been curious about his whereabouts?"

"I see a lot of infidelity in my line of work," Shaw said, his voice a low rumble. "You'd be surprised how many women stick around even when their husband has cheated on them five times before."

"Not too surprised," Fallyn muttered, thinking of her own parents. She sighed and took another bite of her bear claw.

They had tried to contact Emily's old pen pal, but Renee wanted nothing to do with them. Fallyn had left no less than five messages before the pediatrician finally answered.

"Stop calling," she'd said immediately, her tone waspish. "I don't want to be dragged into this ugliness. I'm forty-three and I still have student loans to pay off. Having my name in the paper is the last thing I need."

"We wouldn't—" Fallyn had said, but Renee cut her off.

"I don't know anything else. Leave me alone." And then she hung up.

"I think we've reached the end of the paper trail," Shaw told her now.

All they knew for sure was that Bartholomew was, indeed, living in Bluebird Bay at the time of the incident, that he was older than Emily (like the doctor had said "Barry" was), and that he had gone by Barry back in high school.

It was hardly enough to bring out the pitchforks.

In fact, altogether, it amounted to...a whole pile of nothing.

Fallyn looked down at a picture of a handsome, smiling Chaz Bartholomew in his football uniform, surrounded by a bunch of friends who looked just like him. The kid was wealthy and confident; even in a still image, he looked like he would swagger.

According to Cee-cee, he came off as a nice enough guy...

but spoiled. The sort of kid who got a brand new car as a gift on his sixteenth birthday.

He had the face of a politician. And it was that very thought that had her Spidey senses tingling. Men like that often thought they were above the law.

Ethan called then, and she let the detective go to voicemail. She'd deal with him after she'd finished her bear claw and coffee. When the message came through, she set her phone on Shaw's desk and played it on speakerphone.

"Hi Fallyn, this is Detective Jenkins. I just wanted to let you know that the meeting to discuss potentially reopening Emily's case was rescheduled for next week. I know it's frustrating, but active open cases take precedence. I'm not giving up, okay? Call me back when you can."

Fallyn glared at the phone and took a savage bite of her pastry.

"I can almost hear your brain percolating," Shaw told her, sounding amused. "What are you thinking?"

"I'm not sure you want to know."

Shaw grinned. "I definitely do. Though, I think I already know."

"You think you know me so well already, huh? Okay, then shoot. What am I thinking?"

"You're frustrated they aren't reopening the case and feel like it might never happen," Shaw said, looking her straight in the eye. "You didn't take the call because if we tell him about Chaz, he's going to say we still don't have enough to open the case again. Plus, he also might tell us in no uncertain terms not to contact him. You're looking for plausible deniability."

Fallyn was impressed. He'd guessed it, pretty much verbatim. She cocked a brow at him. "Well, what do you think?" she asked. "Should we follow Steph's lead and ask for forgiveness instead of permission and go get a feel for ol' Chaz?"

"We shouldn't," Shaw said, and disappointment weighed heavy in her stomach. Then, he grinned. "But we will."

Fallyn took another long pull from her coffee and bit back a smile.

Another check mark in the pro column for Private Investigator David Shaw.

22

CEE-CEE

"Hi Mom!" Max ran up to Cee-cee in the restaurant parking lot and pulled her into a tight hug. "Thanks for meeting me here. I know it's a little bit out of the way, but it's *so* worth it."

They were one town up the coast from Bluebird Bay, at a little restaurant called *Stacked*. It was famous for its endless burger combinations. Cee-cee had even seen it featured on the Food Network — which is what she usually had on in the background at home. The place was famous for its lobster burger... though from what Cee-cee had seen, it was just a classic lobster roll in a more burger-y shape.

"It doesn't hurt me to venture out of Bluebird Bay every now and then," Cee-cee laughed. "And it's always fun to try a new restaurant. Especially with my favorite daughter."

"I'm your only daughter," Max protested.

"It's been too long since we did something just you and me."

"Agreed," Max said heartily.

Cee-cee shivered as the wind picked up. "Come on, let's go in."

"Oh! Shoot, I forgot something in the car. Go ahead and get a table. I'll be right there."

Max ran off, and Cee-cee walked into the restaurant. The decorations were reminiscent of a fifties diner, but the decor featured more wood than plastic or chrome. The place was packed, and Cee-cee was still waiting up front when Max came back in carrying two gift bags.

"What's this?" Cee-cee asked in surprise.

"Just a little something for you," Max said coyly. "I know we already had a shower and all, but I wanted to do something just me and you before your big day."

Cee-cee put an arm around her daughter, leaning her head against Max's. "You're just the sweetest."

"Cee-cee, party of two?" a server said brightly. "We have a booth ready for you."

They followed the woman back through the noisy restaurant, past old neon signs and posters of Rosie the Riveter. The decor was all over the place. And so was the music, Cee-cee realized, as it leapt from Elvis Presley to Jake Bugg. But it all worked, somehow. She could see why Max and Ian loved this place.

"Have you been here before?" their server asked as they sat down.

"I have," Max chirped.

"I'll leave you to it. Someone will be by with your water in a few, and you can give them your orders."

"Okay," Max said as the server walked away. She was bright and excited, and for a moment, Cee-cee marveled at how beautiful and grown up her daughter was. Then, she turned her attention to the slip of paper that Max was holding out.

"So you put your orders on these," Max explained. "You choose your bun, patty, sauce, toppings..."

Cee-cee stared down at the list in her hands. There must be a thousand possible combinations. "What are you going to order?"

"I don't know yet. I get something different every time. The sourdough buns are amazing, and the bacon onion jam is *so* good. I'm definitely getting sweet potato fries too. And maybe I'll try the grilled chicken this time..."

Cee-cee studied the menu for a while before she finally checked off her choices: Multigrain Bun, Organic Bison Burger, Smoked Gouda, Horseradish Aioli, Roasted Red Peppers, and Grilled Onions. On the back, she checked her choice of wine. As a busboy came by with their water, she added a check next to Broccoli Sprouts at the last minute — and a side of onion rings too.

"I can see why you keep coming here," she said after they'd handed over their orders. "You could come every day for a year and never get the same thing twice."

"Right?" Max exclaimed. "I love it!"

"What did you get?"

"Grilled chicken on sourdough with pesto. And a bunch of toppings," she added, giggling. "I don't even remember. Artichoke hearts and some other stuff. Herbed goat cheese."

"I have to bring Mick here on our next date night. He'll love it."

"Speaking of Mick!" Max said, grabbing the gift bags and setting them on the table. "Here!"

Cee-cee reached into the slim bag first, knowing that she was going to pull out a book. She recognized the bag as one that Max carried in her shop. What she wasn't expecting was a colorful picture book: *Oh, the Places You'll Go!*

"I used to read this to you and Gabe," Cee-cee said fondly.

"Exactly." Max smiled. "I remember. But that's only part of why I want you to have it. You're starting a whole new life with Mick. And so I wanted to get you something to celebrate all of the good times ahead. And anyway, you can read it to Gracie when she's older."

"It's perfect." Cee-cee reached across the table and squeezed her daughter's hand. "This is lovely, Max. Thank you."

"Take care of it, okay?" Max said with a touch of humor to her voice. "It's worth, like, six hundred dollars."

Cee-cee looked up in surprise, and Max laughed. "Don't worry. I didn't pay that. I didn't pay anything for it, really. I was buying boxes of books at an estate sale and they threw this one in for nothing."

This copy looked even older than the one she'd had when her kids were small; it was faded and the corners were worn. She opened the book and realized that it was a first edition copy.

"You should sell it," Cee-cee told her, offering the book back.

"No! It's yours."

"That's a lot of money."

"You have no idea. Some of the books I found at that sale are worth over two thousand dollars, and there are dozens of them. Honestly, Mom, that's the only reason I've made a profit this year. It has nothing to do with the bookshop. It's the rare books I've been selling online. The bookshop doesn't make much financial sense... I just love it. Being surrounded by books all day, *talking* about books all day. And as long as it's not *losing* me money..." Max shrugged.

"It makes my heart soar to see you so happy, Max. And I'm proud of you for choosing happiness over a lucrative career. Not many people are that wise. They're always so busy chasing the next big thing that they never stop to enjoy everything they *have*."

"I'm proud of you too, Mom. I love seeing you so strong, taking command of your life." Her expression turned serious. "It makes me wish that you hadn't wasted all those years with Dad."

Cee-cee grabbed her hand again. "Max, no! That wasn't a waste. I got twenty beautiful years with you and Gabe. I got to be with you every minute when you were learning to walk and talk. I got to go to your school plays and sew your Halloween costumes and bake cupcakes with you... it was everything I ever wanted. I'm so glad I got to spend those years as a full-time mom. Your dad has his faults, but he always provided for us. That's what gave me the freedom and support I needed to be the mother I wanted to be."

"Yeah," Max said somewhat reluctantly. "I appreciate that. I just wish you had been able to focus a little bit more on what made *you* happy."

"*You* made me happy," Cee-cee insisted. "You and Gabe. You still do."

"You know what I mean, Mom. All those years wearing clothes that weren't really *you*, eating food you didn't really like, socializing with Dad's coworkers." She shook her head and smiled. "But you're happy now. You've created a phenomenal life for yourself, and that's what we're celebrating tonight."

"Cheers to that." Cee-cee picked up the glass of wine that a stealthy server had left on the table while she and Max were deep in conversation.

"Cheers," Max said with a smile. She picked up her pint of pale ale and clinked it gently against Cee-cee's wine glass. They drank, and Max's face took on a thoughtful expression.

"Everything you went through with Dad gives me the motivation to make sure I get it right the first time. That I choose the right person — and even then, that I never give a man complete control over my life. You and Mick showed me that I need someone who *complements* me — not someone who completes me. Does that make sense?"

"That makes complete sense," Cee-cee said approvingly. "And you're off to a great start with Ian."

"He's pretty perfect," Max said, grinning down at the table. Then, her grin faltered and she looked back up at her mother. "Were you ever happy with Dad?"

"Sure I was," she said. "Those early days were hard, but they were beautiful too. We were so excited when we bought our first house, back when I was pregnant with Gabe. And when you two were little, he spent every weekend with us. We'd slather you with sunscreen or bundle you up in wool and spend the whole day out on his boat. Just the four of us, way out on the water. It was magic. There were good days too, sweetheart. So many good days."

"Most of them were before I can remember, I guess."

It hurt Cee-cee's heart to hear that. Nate and Max had *adored* each other in those early years. But they had grown so far apart. She felt sad for both of her children that they didn't have a stronger relationship with their father. Pop may have been ornery, but he and his daughters had loved each other with their whole hearts. She knew that Nate felt the same way about his children... he was just terrible at expressing it or connecting with them in a meaningful way.

"Have you spent any time with your dad lately?" she asked, trying to sound casual.

"Yeah, I met him for lunch a couple days ago. He was only half there, but what else is new. He's always thinking about work. And I think he's not crazy about you getting married... probably just wants it to be over with."

Cee-cee nodded. "That's understandable."

She hoped that's all it was...

Max wrinkled her nose and said, "Forget about him. He's a grownup, and he has to learn to take ownership of his own choices. Let's focus on the here and now. Open your other present!"

Cee-cee had nearly forgotten about the large second gift bag. What could that possibly be? Inside the paper bag was a rectangular basket, like a picnic basket. And inside of the basket was an array of treats. There were truffles, fancy chocolates, candied ginger, figs, pistachios... and some odd things too. Health supplements? Max had included saffron, fenugreek-ginko tea, and red ginseng. There was even a tin of smoked oysters. She was looking at Cee-cee with an expectant smirk, like there was a joke her mother hadn't been clued in on yet.

"Thank you," Cee-cee said uncertainly, and Max's smile widened at her confusion.

"They're aphrodisiacs!" she said. "For your honeymoon!"

Heat rose to Cee-cee's cheeks and she closed the basket, glancing at the table next to them. "Max!"

"Honeymoons aren't what they used to be," Max lamented, her eyes sparkling with humor, "what with couples living in sin and all. So I thought I'd give you some treats to turn things up a notch."

Cee-cee laughed, the blush of embarrassment still burning on her cheeks. "We don't have time for a honeymoon."

"But you're going away for a few days after the wedding, right? Make the most of it!" Max straightened as she spotted their food approaching the table. "Finally! I'm starved."

Cee-cee smiled and shook her head as she placed the basket on the seat next to her. She felt so lucky to be able to share these moments with her daughter, so grateful that they were still so close and that Max had moved home to Bluebird Bay.

Max was right, and so was Mick. She needed to stop thinking about Nate and focus on the present, because the present was oh so sweet.

23

FALLYN

It was the end of the day by the time they reached the Bartholomew property, a few miles inland from Bluebird Bay. The long driveway leading up to their property was basically a road of its own, with expansive pastures on one side and an old apple orchard on the other. Fallyn spotted four gorgeous palominos out in the field; their coats shone like gold in the light of the sun that hung just above the tops of the shadowy evergreens. There was a massive stable near the house and other shiny new outbuildings. As they reached the end of the driveway, she caught sight of a dilapidated old barn in the back, at the edge of the woods.

The town tax records showed that this place had been in the Bartholomew family for generations. Chaz Bartholomew's parents had given it to him and his wife Nancy as a wedding gift. Even so, the upkeep and maintenance on this place must cost a fortune.

As they walked up to the house, the front door was opened by an older version of the man that they had been scrutinizing in photos all day. He was a bit paunchier than he had been in high school, but still a good-looking guy. His hair was darker than ever; it looked like he dyed it.

"Can I help you?" he asked, flashing them a dental-ad smile. His teeth were an unnatural shade of white. When Chaz looked from Shaw to Fallyn, his smile faltered slightly and his cheeks lost some of their color.

He recognized her.

Shaw stiffened beside her, and she knew that he realized it too.

Before Fallyn could introduce herself, Chaz said, "I saw your picture in the paper. You're the reporter who found that poor woman's remains in the bay. What an awful thing." He shook his head and then gestured for them to follow him inside. "Come in, come in."

The front door opened into a massive foyer, one of those waste-of-space rooms that was nothing but marble and air with an elaborate staircase at the back. He walked straight through to a sitting room — passing two other living rooms on the way — and gestured for them to sit down on a leather sofa. They did so, Fallyn perching nervously on the edge of the seat.

Chaz had his back to them, pouring three drinks from a crystal decanter. He wore tan slacks and an expensive-looking sweater, and there was an anxiety in his movements that he had managed to keep out of his voice.

"Barry?" a woman called. Fallyn's heart sped when she heard the nickname. Next to Fallyn, Shaw froze. "Whose car is that?"

A moment later, Nancy walked into the room. When she glanced at Fallyn and Shaw on the couch, her face looked pale — but this was Maine in early spring, Fallyn reminded herself. Everyone was either pale or an orangish sort of fake-tan. She was dressed like she was on her way to a board meeting, with crisp slacks and a white shirt.

When Fallyn was home alone, she wore an oversized shirt and huge gray sweatpants that looked like elephant legs. But hey — just because she couldn't relate to these people didn't mean Chaz Bartholomew was a murderer.

So why was every nerve in her body screaming *DANGER?*

He offered her a glass of something amber-colored and she took it... with no intention of taking so much as a sip.

Nancy was staring at her husband, waiting for an answer to her question.

"This is Fallyn Rappaport," he said in a smooth voice, "and her friend...?"

"David Shaw, private investigator," Shaw introduced himself. "We're trying to find answers for Emily's family. There's nothing to be found on paper or online, and so we've been speaking to longtime residents of Bluebird Bay."

Nancy shook her head and crossed her arms over her stomach. "What a terrible thing to find. And her poor mother... I can't even imagine. We just have the one child, grown now, and he is the light of our life."

"It's been hard on her," Shaw said in a low, soothing tone. "We're hoping to bring her some closure."

"Of course. I see my husband has furnished you with drinks but maybe you'd care for coffee or tea instead?"

"Actually, I'd love a cup of coffee," Shaw said.

"Fallyn?" Nancy asked.

"Sure, I'll take a cup of coffee," Fallyn managed. "Thank you."

"Of course." Nancy walked out of the room, still clutching her own arms like she was trying to hold herself together.

Barry sat down across from them and took a long sip of his drink. "I can only guess you being here together has something to do with this case, but I'm wracking my brain and I can't imagine what. I didn't know the Addison family — at least, not better than anyone else in Bluebird Bay."

Shaw looked to Fallyn, letting her take the lead. She needed to tread carefully. Aside from Barry recognizing her, she hadn't picked up on any red flags.

"Like Shaw said, we're speaking to everyone we can to try to piece together information about Emily. We're hoping to get more information on where she spent her free time, and with whom. And so we've been seeking out anyone who knew her, went to school with her... or frequented the pharmacy she worked at."

Barry raised his eyebrows and nodded slowly. "Well, I did know her in passing. I was a pretty regular customer at the pharmacy, so I knew all the clerks. She seemed like a nice enough woman."

Woman. That was the second time he had referred to Emily as such. That in and of itself felt like a glaring red flag to Fallyn... but maybe she was reading too much into things.

"In Emily's journal," she said, taking a chance, "she wrote that an older man was coming into the pharmacy and flirting with her. Did you ever see anything like that?"

She could have sworn that she saw a flash of violence in Barry's eyes — but when he spoke, his voice was calm and level. "I can't say I did."

There was a loud whirring sound in the distance and he said, "That's just Nancy grinding our coffee."

"Did you ever see anyone hanging around Emily at work?" Shaw asked.

"*I* didn't work there." His voice had a slight edge of irritation to it now. "I wasn't hanging around. I was only ever passing through for a pack of cigarettes — back before I quit," he added, smiling at Nancy as she walked into the room. She was carrying a silver tray loaded with four glass mugs, cream and sugar, and coffee still in a French press.

"Thank you," Fallyn said as Nancy poured the coffee.

"Of course. You must have had a long day. I can only imagine how many residents you've interviewed."

"Just doing our due diligence," Shaw rumbled.

Nancy pressed a hand to her temple. "I'm going to go upstairs, if you don't mind. Just seeing that news story in the paper gave me nightmares — we installed a whole new security system and everything. It's horrible to think of something like that happening so close to home. I can't listen to anything more about it."

"Of course," said Shaw. "Thank you for the coffee."

Nancy walked out, and no one so much as glanced at the coffee that sat waiting on the tray.

"So you never noticed anyone paying any special attention to Emily?" Fallyn asked Barry.

"I've already told you, no." His voice wasn't so calm and level now. "I hardly noticed her. I only knew her name because of her little plastic name tag. I try to treat employees like they're people, you know? Heck, I was raised by a string of nannies. I call people by name, that's all. Remind them they're human. Show them *I* know they're people, I mean."

Fallyn wasn't sure what to say to that. Barry had caught himself blathering, and now he sat with his mouth shut in a thin line. She schooled her face into a neutral expression and asked, "Did you ever see Emily outside of the pharmacy?"

The look in Barry's eyes was fierce, his voice low and level. "Are you asking if I was sleeping with her?"

Fallyn's mouth dropped open. "I didn't—"

He laughed; it was a grating sound. "That's ridiculous. Are you planning to ask every customer at the pharmacy the same questions? Why don't you go back to Chicago and report on a real crime?"

Fallyn felt a hot flash of anger. She kept her voice level when she asked, "Is murder not a 'real crime' in your mind?"

"I mean a crime that happened in this century." He turned to Shaw with a scathing look. "What kind of two-bit PI are you? Trying to up your hourly by going door to door, talking to every single person who lived in Bluebird Bay when that woman disappeared?"

Shaw didn't reply.

"This was a mistake," Barry said. "You should leave."

Fallyn set down the glass she held and stood. Barry showed them the door, and she and Shaw walked out. As she opened the car door, she could feel Barry's eyes on her back. Inside the car, Shaw asked, "What do you think?"

"I don't like him. Not one bit." She sighed and slumped back in her seat. "The thing is, we don't have anything on him."

"That's the long and the short of it," Shaw said, looking thoughtful.

"But Shaw, his wife called him *Barry*."

Shaw nodded as he started the car. "And it was super odd that he kept calling Emily a woman."

"Right?" She turned to look at him. "That was so creepy."

As Shaw drove around the circular top of the driveway, Fallyn caught sight of that old barn again. It was half-covered in weeds and surrounded by young trees, like they were deliberately letting it be swallowed by the forest.

"Do you think that's weird?" she asked.

"What's weird?"

"The barn," she said, pointing. "Everything else is picture perfect, like a magazine. The landscaping, the house, her hair and clothes — hell, even the horses look gold plated. Everything on this property is totally Stepford... except for that barn. Why leave that dilapidated old outbuilding? It just feels off to me."

Driving ten miles per hour, Shaw bent forward and peered at the barn. Then, he leaned back and let out a sigh. "I can't say I don't agree."

"So what are we gonna do about it?" she asked, her senses humming.

"We do what we're good at," he said evenly. "We investigate."

24

FALLYN

This wasn't smart. She knew it. Shaw knew it.

And still, here they were, skulking through the woods towards a creaky old barn that just felt out of place. Shaw had parked his car on a country road behind the Bartholomew home, where a thick stretch of woods separated their property from the street.

At the start of her career in investigative journalism, Fallyn had put zero stock in the term "gut feeling". But by the end of it, she knew without a doubt that her instincts were her greatest asset. So when Shaw agreed without question, it felt like they were kindred spirits.

He led the way, holding a flashlight he kept in his car. He had it on the lowest setting, shedding just enough light to keep them from tripping over logs and fallen branches on the forest floor. The man had a steady sense of direction; when they reached the edge of the woods, they were even with the barn. Shaw turned off his flashlight as they neared the overgrown field.

"Plenty big enough for a boat," Shaw mused as they

hunkered down near the tree line. Fallyn edged away from a patch of poison ivy and crouched shoulder to shoulder with Shaw, peering at the back of the barn in the fading twilight.

"Should we go check it out?" she asked.

Shaw looked from the house to the barn. "If we cross here, we'll be visible from the back windows of the house. But I don't see anywhere we'd be completely hidden."

"The house has a hundred windows," Fallyn said. "What are the chances they'll glance outside right then?"

"Our visit put them on edge," he replied. "It's risky. If we get caught and the Bartholomews call the police, we'll get sidelined for the remainder of the investigation. Depending on who shows up, they could even arrest us. I wouldn't put it past these people to press charges."

She shook her head. "No. They wouldn't want to draw attention to themselves."

"We should at least wait until it's fully dark," Shaw said.

"You're right." Fallyn walked back into the trees a ways and pulled her phone out of her pocket. "I'm going to text Detective Jenkins."

I'm with Shaw near the Bartholomew property, she told the detective. *We believe he's the Barry that Emily wrote about, and we think there may be evidence in the barn. Can you come check it out?*

Triple dots appeared almost immediately as Ethan replied. A text came through saying: *It will take time to get a warrant. If we can get one at all. Go on home and I'll question Barry tomorrow. I'm dealing with a back-road collision right now.*

She knew he was right — but at the same time, she felt sick at the thought of waiting that long. They had pushed too hard and put the couple on edge. Had they botched it? What if the Bartholomews moved whatever it was they were hiding before the cops could get a warrant? Because they were hiding *something* in that old barn. Fallyn could feel it in her bones.

She made her way back to the edge of the woods, where Shaw was still peering out into the gloom.

"Ethan says to go home and he'll follow up in the morning, try to get a warrant."

"He has to say that," Shaw muttered. "He's a cop."

"What do you want to do?"

Shaw turned to look at her, eyes dark in the shadows of the trees. In a gentle voice, he asked, "Do you want to leave?"

"No," she said immediately.

A smile flitted across his face and he turned back to the barn. "Then we stay. We'll wait here until it's fully dark and —" Shaw stiffened and stopped speaking mid-sentence.

She followed his gaze and spotted Chaz Bartholomew walking quickly across the overgrown field that separated the barn from the rest of the property. He was moving with agitated, jerky movements, kicking at clumps of brush.

She turned to Shaw in shock. He gave her a quick, wide-eyed glance before turning back to Barry. The man pulled a key from his pocket and used it to open the rusty old padlock that held the barn doors closed. He hurried inside and pulled the doors closed behind him.

"Well, that's not suspicious at all," Shaw said softly.

Fallyn's pulse thrummed rapidly through her neck and wrists, and she fought to keep her breathing slow and steady. If she wasn't sure before, she was now. There was something in that barn.

"If we wait," she murmured, "whatever he's trying to hide could be moved or destroyed." She paused. "I don't want to drag you into something dangerous, but I have to go in there."

"No need to drag me," said Shaw, eyes on the barn. "I'm in."

"Okay," she breathed, relief washing over her.

"I'll do the talking," she told him, thinking out loud. "I'll try to defuse the situation... maybe say that I forgot to ask him one last thing. And we saw him headed out to the barn, so we followed him. If he's doing something wrong... well, he won't ask questions unless he has nothing to hide, because he'll want to pretend like everything's fine. He's not going to freak out and grill us. That would make him look guilty."

Shaw shot her an incredulous look, but he didn't argue. He just rose to his feet and strode across the clearing towards the barn, skirting the patch of poison ivy. Fallyn's phone buzzed in her pocket; she muted it with a click and followed Shaw.

He opened the barn door cautiously. Inside, Barry was fiddling with an old burnt-out light bulb. Another light closer to the doors was on, and Fallyn watched the man's face pale when he spotted them. A split second later, he plastered that dental-ad smile back onto his face.

"I thought you folks had gone home." There was no hint of stress or strain in Barry's voice. The man deserved an Oscar.

"We stopped to speak to another long-time resident on our way back," Fallyn told him, "and our conversation with them raised more questions than it answered. We wanted to come back and speak to you while we were still in the neighborhood. When we drove up, we saw you walking out to the barn and so we followed. I hope that's okay."

"Yes, of course. We keep odd hours here. The work on a property this size never really ends, you know. Who were you talking to?"

"I'm afraid I can't reveal my sources," Fallyn told him.

Barry's eyes narrowed. "Are you writing an article on this? I thought you were just looking for answers for the Addison family."

"No article," Fallyn said. "Still, I keep my conversations confidential. I'm sure you can appreciate that."

The old light bulb flicked to life behind him, fully illuminating the dank, dusty space.

Fallyn kept talking, only half listening to herself as she spun a story about what they had heard from a neighbor, about Emily hanging out with an unsavory crowd from out of town.

No boat, she noted with a sense of disappointment. Just a covered old car and lots of old crates and boxes that might have something hidden inside.

"Did you notice anyone strange hanging around the pharmacy?" As Fallyn spoke, Shaw edged almost imperceptibly towards the car. "Any out of towners? Reports say that they were in their early twenties and wore all black."

"As I told you before, I don't remember anyone hanging around that store. It was a very long time ago, and I was never there just hanging around outside."

"Yes, I understand," Fallyn said, watching Shaw from the corner of her eye. "That's too bad. Thank you for your cooperation. We'll have to see if anyone else remembers someone fitting that description."

Shaw lifted up the corner of the canvas that covered the car, and Fallyn caught a glimpse of bright red paint. The color hit her like a blow to the head, and it took a moment for her to remember why.

Candy Apple Red!! Emily had written.

The car that had gone missing when Emily did, never to be found.

The reason so many people said that she must have run away from home.

Fallyn's breath caught in her chest. If that *was* Emily's car, Barry was a cornered animal. They were both in terrible danger. Shaw let the canvas drop, shooting Fallyn a significant look. Barry turned to look at him, and Fallyn distracted him with an explosive sneeze.

"Sorry," she murmured when Barry jumped. Shaw appeared back at her side. "My allergies hate dust."

Barry shot her a sparkling smile. "We'd best get you out of here, then. Let's talk back up at the house. Or if you've gotten all you need to, I can walk you back to your car?"

"No one's going anywhere," Nancy said.

Fallyn spun around to see Barry's wife standing in the door of the barn.

Nancy raised a shotgun to her shoulder and pointed it at Shaw.

"There's no car in the driveway, Barry," Nancy said without taking her eyes off of the PI. "These people were sneaking around our land in the dark."

Nancy glanced at Fallyn, and her blood ran cold at the crazy in the woman's eyes.

"What are you doing?" Barry asked his wife. His tone

was gentle, placating, and Fallyn could imagine him talking that way to a skittish horse. "Don't do this, Nance."

"They know," she snapped. "And if you don't realize that, you're an idiot."

"I don't know what—" Fallyn began, and Nancy turned the gun on her.

"Shut up! It's enough that you're sneaking around our barn in the dark. I'd be perfectly within my rights to shoot the both of you."

"Not in Maine," Shaw told her, his voice a low rumble.

Nancy swung the gun back towards him. "Tie them up, Barry."

"And then what?" he asked with a tremor in his voice. "What are we going to do with them?"

"I'll figure it out," Nancy growled. "I always do. *Now*, Barry."

Barry picked up a frayed length of rope and walked towards Shaw.

"You don't have to do this," Shaw told him quietly.

Barry didn't meet his eyes. "Hands behind your back."

Shaw obeyed, eyes on the gun.

Nancy paced back and forth in the doorway, muttering under her breath. Fallyn scanned the barn for something she could use as a weapon. There was a pitchfork a few feet away. She looked back towards the shotgun. Or was it a rifle? Could it kill her at close range?

Fallyn gulped. Maybe if she distracted Nancy with talk, she'd get a chance to disarm her.

"So it was you?" Fallyn asked. "You found out that your husband was sleeping with Emily, and you killed her in a jealous rage?"

Nancy shot her a scornful look.

"Or did he do this and convince you to clean up his mess?"

Nancy barked a laugh at that and brought the gun back up to her shoulder. "He doesn't have the guts."

"So you did it?" Fallyn asked again.

"*Emily* did this!" Nancy shouted. "*Emily* slept with a married man while his *wife* was in and out of the *hospital*. All through my first trimester, I couldn't keep any food down. And what does this miserable excuse for a man do? He finds a side piece. But did she stay in the shadows? No! *Emily* came into this house and told me that she was pregnant. She said that she was going to *keep* it and name Barry as the father." She let out another harsh laugh. "The *nerve*."

"So you killed her?"

Nancy's eyes were hard. "I did what I had to do to protect my son." Something fragile and frightened flickered through her eyes as she said, "I was just trying to keep her from leaving — from ruining our lives. I only meant to knock her out, buy myself some more time. What else could I do? She was still in high school. People would have called Barry a pedophile. It would have ruined his business. It would have ruined my son's life before he was even born. All because that homewrecker couldn't keep her legs closed. Who knows if he was even the father? He was just the richest guy she'd slept with that month. She was trying to shake us down, threaten everything we had built, everything we had to offer our son!"

"Nance," Barry said in that same gentling tone, "I'm sorry. You know that. I'm so sorry. But this isn't the way. We can't just keep—"

"We can and we will," Nancy snapped. "It's the only

way. You make me sick, you know that? You can commit the most heinous acts of betrayal with a smile on your face, but when it comes time to man up and protect your family, you get squeamish."

She spit on the floor at his feet, the gun moving off target, and Fallyn saw her chance. She dived for the pitchfork. Shaw saw her and lunged towards Barry, keeping the attention on him. His hands were bound, so he went for Barry headfirst, driving his skull into Barry's nose.

Fallyn lunged, aiming the pitchfork for Nancy's thigh... and then the gun went off.

Sparks of pain seared Fallyn's shoulder, but she kept her grip on the pitchfork. The rusty tool went easily through the other woman's linen pants, and Nancy screamed. Fallyn grabbed the barrel of the gun, still hot against her skin, and wrenched it from Nancy's hands.

When she turned, Shaw had Barry in a headlock. He had managed to break through the tattered rope that Barry had used to bind his wrists — either that, or Barry was crap at knots. Fallyn turned back to Nancy and leveled the shotgun at her chest.

Shaw tied Barry up, hopefully doing a better job of it than the other man had, then crossed the barn and ripped the dusty canvas cover off of the car.

It was a boxy old Volkswagen Rabbit. Candy-apple red.

Sirens sounded in the distance as her phone began to buzz. She kept one hand on the shotgun and reached into her pocket with the other, wincing as fresh pain shot through her injured shoulder.

"I've been trying to reach you," said Ethan tersely. "I'm a half mile away. Can I turn these sirens off or what?"

Fallyn met Nancy's eyes and said, "Or what." She dropped the phone and returned both hands to the shotgun.

She wasn't sure what hurt more: her shoulder or the thought of the reaming they were about to get from the local detective. But as she glanced at the car and pictured Emily behind the wheel, sixteen and smiling, she knew that it was all worth it.

25

FALLYN

She breathed deep, relishing the tang of the sea air as Gabe's boat soared across the gentle chop of the ocean waves. It was early still; they had a few hours before Gabe had to be back on land for his mom's big day. The sun was warm on Fallyn's face, her body snug in a dry neoprene wetsuit.

The Bartholomews were both in custody. They hadn't been officially convicted yet — but as far as the good people of Bluebird Bay were concerned, they had already been tried and found guilty. The town had gotten the closure that it needed the day that the Bartholomews appeared in the local paper.

Everyone but Patty Addison.

For her, the news took longer to sink in. When Fallyn went to the Addison house that first morning to break the news, Patty had still been fretting over Emily.

"It's getting late," she told Fallyn, "and she still hasn't called. I knew I shouldn't have gotten her that car. But oh, you should have seen the look on her face when she saw it." Patty's face brightened and she relaxed. "She'll be alright.

She's a good girl. I'll send Joey out to look for her if she's not home soon. She could have at least called me..."

They had tried more than once to tell her what had happened, but their words had fallen on deaf ears. Her caretaker, Kathleen, assured Fallyn that the news would sink in eventually. Sooner or later, Patty would have a lucid moment, and she would tell her then. Fallyn left feeling heartsick for the old woman, hoping that the news would bring Emily's mother a bit of peace.

Though, she supposed that it was just as well if Patty remained oblivious to the court proceedings that might stretch out all spring and even through the summertime.

The Bartholomews had yet to confess, and no one knew how they had disposed of Emily's body. Had there been a third accomplice?

In Fallyn's experience, sooner or later, the code of ethics that bonded criminals (and couples) broke down in the face of more lenient sentences. They'd be turning on each other like caged dogs soon enough, and the rest of the story would come to light sooner or later.

The Bluebird Bay police force had appeared on the scene just minutes after Fallyn spoke to Ethan on the phone. When she hadn't replied to his texts, he knew that she was going in. He had left the scene of the accident he'd been attending to in order to drive to the Bartholomew house.

"Call it gut instinct," he'd said as the couple sat in the back of his squad car.

News had spread quickly, and there had been a lovely memorial for Emily the day before. She had been interred earlier that month, but the closure that Fallyn and Shaw had brought to her case inspired the town to turn out and honor her properly. Maryanne had organized a graveside memorial service and adorned Emily's final resting place with a hundred daisy chains.

That was the day it finally sank in for Patty. Fallyn, Shaw, Alex, and Maryanne had gathered at the Addison house just before the service to tell her again that Emily's killer had been caught. At first, she hadn't seemed to understand. And then, she had started to cry.

"Emily's home," Patty said at last. "She's home with Joey. She can finally rest."

She had thanked them all…Alex first, and then the rest of them. She had even hugged Fallyn and thanked her for bringing Emily home to Bluebird Bay so that she could rest beside her brother.

The whole town showed up for Emily's memorial — or so it seemed to Fallyn, who was surprised that Bluebird Bay could turn out a crowd like that one — and it was cathartic to see Patty Addison surrounded by so much love and support. Old friends apologized for long absences; they made plans to visit and play bridge.

Fallyn hoped that Patty could enjoy whatever time she had left. Lord knew she deserved it. And she would see her children again soon enough.

"Look!" Gabe called, pulling Fallyn's attention back to the scene in front of her. Off to their left, whales were breaching the surface of the water. Their immense bodies seemed to hang in midair before returning to the sea with a splash.

"What did I miss?" Shaw walked up from below, stiff and slow in his thick neoprene wetsuit. "I'm as quick and graceful as a walrus in this thing."

Shaw had scolded Fallyn soundly when he'd learned that she had gone scuba diving without a partner. Having a dive buddy who could help you if something went awry was the primary rule of scuba — but of course, Fallyn hadn't known anyone crazy enough to dive the Gulf of Maine with her this time of year.

"When you dive alone," he'd said seriously, quoting the old adage, "you die alone. What if you ran out of air and there was no one there to spot you?"

Today would be their third dive together. He had approached their first dive with a certain stoicism ("They say ice baths are good for your health.") but had been surprisingly eager to plan their next trip into the deep. The company itself would have been good enough, but he was really getting into the spirit of things. They had stayed at Mo's Diner past closing the night before, poring over the maps and ships logs that Fallyn had collected that winter.

"Whales," Fallyn said. "Look!"

More whales came up for breath, and she could hear the *whoosh* from their blowholes.

"Amazing," he said. He stood close enough to Fallyn that his arm touched hers.

"This is the spot," Gabe announced as the boat drifted to a stop.

Fallyn looked up into a pair of eyes that had become increasingly familiar to her lately. Today, they were the same gray as the sea. And like the ocean, she knew that there was so much more just beneath the surface.

"Ready, Shaw?"

"Call me David," he said, voice low enough that only she could hear him. "Please."

Fallyn smiled at him. "Are you ready, David?"

He just grinned and shouldered his air tanks. He checked that everything was in place, then fell backwards over the side.

Fallyn found him waiting for her just below the surface, and they descended together. Treasure hunt aside, she had fallen in love with the freedom of diving. An entire underwater world just to themselves.

Shaw — David — caught her attention with a wave of his gloved hand, and she followed him to a rocky expanse covered in a constellation of fire-colored sea stars. Fallyn grinned so wide that she nearly lost her regulator. Crabs and lobsters skittered here and there. She and David hung still for a while, watching them. Fallyn enjoyed the feeling of weightlessness, of being in this place outside of space and time with a dive partner who was never in a rush.

She thought of Emily every time she dove. She supposed she always would. But she realized now that finding Emily Addison had been a blessing.

Fallyn had come to Bluebird Bay to find treasure... and she had. She had brought Emily home to her mother, and that was worth more than any gold.

A motion pulled her gaze to the right, and she kicked slowly with her fins. There was a plume of sand coming up from the sea floor, and as she moved closer to investigate, a startled fish shot up in a blur of motion and rushed away.

Fallyn was just turning to go back the way she had come when a winking light caught her eye. She reached down through the sandy water and fumbled clumsily with her gloved hand. Finally, her fingers closed around something hard. Could it possibly be...?

It was. A coin. How old, she couldn't tell in this murky blue light. But when she rooted around in the same spot, she found two more. David hung in mid-water nearby, watching her. When she held them up for him to see, his eyes crinkled joyfully behind the glass of his mask. Bubbles poured from his mouth and he gave her a double thumbs up.

When they surfaced a few minutes later, Fallyn immediately held the coins up to see them in the sunlight. Despite their tarnished surfaces, they gleamed. She looked closer, trying to make out the details, but she couldn't make out much. Back on land, she would clean them and compare them to other pieces; she had hundreds of photos saved on her laptop.

Could this be a part of the treasure she'd come looking for? They certainly looked the part.

David was already on the boat; he reached down now to give her a hand up. The moment Fallyn got the heavy dive tanks off of her back, David picked her up and spun her around.

"You did it!" he said, more excited than she had ever seen him. Fallyn laughed and leaned in for a hug, feeling warm despite the frigid temperature of the ocean water.

She would stick around and finish her hunt, after all.

Because, who knew... there might be more treasure to be found in Bluebird Bay, after all.

26

CEE-CEE

Cee-cee's hands trembled as she clutched her wildflower bouquet, and she made an effort to loosen her grip. Her whole body seemed to vibrate with anticipation, and she could hardly stand still.

It was finally happening.

She was walking down the aisle to stand beside the love of her life and say her vows. In all the hubbub of getting ready for the wedding these past weeks, while still running their two businesses, she felt as if she had barely seen Mick at all.

She couldn't wait to see him now.

The music started up — Cee-cee had planned on using a recording for simplicity's sake, but Steph had surprised her with a string quartet led by Todd's girlfriend, Alice. It was a beautiful song, slow and soulful but still full of joy.

Alice was such a dear — she must have played three dozen different melodies for Cee-cee before they had decided on this one. She was playing for free, and Todd had paid the other three members of the quartet. It was their wedding gift to Cee-cee and Mick.

"Almost time," Gabe said.

She turned to look up at her son, so handsome in his pale green dress shirt.

He smiled. "Are you ready?"

She smiled back at him. "More than ready."

"You look amazing, Mom."

"Beautiful," Max agreed. *She* looked beautiful in a pale golden pantsuit. It was the sort of garment that would look utterly ridiculous on most people. But Max? Max looked like a princess.

Cee-cee glanced down at the cream-colored slip dress that brushed her ankles. The moment she had tried this dress on, she had known it was the one. It made her feel beautiful. Not young, not old. Just beautiful. And just like herself. It was simple and slinky, something that the old repressed Cee-cee never would have worn. Her hair fell in loose waves over her shoulders, and her sisters had woven flowers into thin braids that wound around her head.

She turned to Anna, who held Teddy under one arm and clutched a basket of flowers in the other, keeping them separate until the last minute. Cee-cee wiggled her eyebrows at her baby sister.

"It's go time, kiddo."

Anna beamed. She set Teddy down in the doorway and whispered, "Okay, sweetpea. Let's go sprinkle the flowers!"

"Spinker fowers!" Teddy chirped, grabbing the basket. He went running down the aisle on chubby little legs, throwing the flowers here and there. Anna ran ahead of him to walk backwards down the aisle, snapping photos as she went

Then, Teddy noticed the people who stood watching him, and he began offering flowers to everyone he passed. Anna guided him onward, and he dumped the last of the flowers at Mick's feet. Then, he put the basket on his head like a hat.

Cee-cee peeked out from the doorway and chuckled. Nate would have hated that, but Mick just watched the boy with a broad smile and a kind word. Tears of gratitude sprang to Cee-cee's eyes. He looked so handsome in a cream-colored linen suit. Relaxed and excited.

He was perfect. Today was perfect.

She was ready.

The string quartet shifted into something that was reminiscent of the bridal march but also entirely unique. Something new.

For a brief, bittersweet moment, Cee-cee wished that her mom and Pop could be here to witness this. Her mom would have loved Mick, would have been giddy with happiness to see the life that Cee-cee had made for herself. She would love to have Pop here to walk her down the aisle one last time. But having Gabe and Max do the honors was just as special.

Cee-cee sent a mental *I love you* to both of her parents and took a deep breath. She wouldn't cry today. At least, not yet.

She looked up at Gabe, standing tall and proud at her left shoulder, and then looked right, into Max's eyes. They were both beaming, and their happiness intensified Cee-cee's threefold. She held her wildflower bouquet in front of her. Each of her children put a hand beneath one of her elbows, and together they walked her down the aisle as her family and Mick's family looked on.

One big family, now.

His cousins nudged each other and murmured under their breath, looking impressed. Steph's son Jeff — now Mick's trusted apprentice — stood arm in arm with his sister, Sarah. Her husband Oliver hadn't been able to make it, but that was all right. Having her niece there filled her heart.

Ethan wrapped his arms around Steph as they watched Cee-cee walk past. Sasha grinned and gave a little wave over Gracie's head; the newest member of their family was fast asleep on her mother's shoulder. Teddy came sprinting back down the aisle, flower basket down over his eyes, and his grandfather scooped him out of the way with an apologetic grin.

Cee-cee set a brisk pace, and her kids kept up. She saw the amusement on Anna's face as she snapped away with her camera and knew that her baby sister would tease her later for rushing down the aisle instead of maintaining a more graceful glide.

Nate would have hated that too — her pace and nearly everything else that made this day so special. She hated that he kept coming into her head, but she couldn't help but compare this wedding to the one she had shared with him, so long ago. That wedding had been formal and opulent, and Cee-cee had been wracked with nerves.

She had been a different person then. So had he. But that was it. Halfway up the aisle, Cee-cee promised herself that she wouldn't think of her ex-husband again.

Not today.

She met Mick's gaze and immediately had to blink back

tears of happiness. Her groom radiated love, and the joy lighting his eyes looked like rays of sunshine.

The ceremony was short and sweet, and their handwritten vows, even sweeter. Tears streamed down her face as her husband bent her backwards and kissed her. His scent enveloped her, and, for a moment, it was just the two of them as the rest of the world disappeared.

When he pulled away, she was breathless.

And, just like that, Mick was her husband. The man she would spend the rest of her life with.

With a start, Cee-cee realized that their entire family was clapping and cheering. She tore her eyes from Mick's face and turned towards the crowd, including everyone in their joy. The crowd parted — they had simply stood in place for the short ceremony, and there were no tables to move — and the aisle widened and transformed into a dance floor.

Alice and her band struck up a new song, and Mick and Cee-cee went straight into their first dance. Nothing slow and stately for them, no. This was a celebration! And Mick was a fantastic dancer. Alice's fingers danced and her bow flew across her fiddle as Mick twirled Cee-cee around and around across the wooden floor. She found herself laughing from the sheer joy of it all, and Mick joined in. Soon their family joined them on the dance floor, and Cee-cee felt surrounded by love.

Eventually, the string quartet turned folk band took a break. Ian set up the tiny, powerful sound system he had brought, and Max started up a playlist she had made with Mick and Cee-cee's favorite songs. There was a fantastic buffet from Monzano's with lasagna, fettuccini, tiramisu... all of the things that Cee-cee had denied herself for years. The festivities felt positively hedonistic, and she loved every minute of them.

It wasn't until Cee-cee paused to eat that she really took in the decorations. Her sisters had done a phenomenal job. The wooden tables along one wall were set with elaborate driftwood centerpieces and strewn with bits of sea glass. There were wildflowers everywhere — the tables, the walls, people's hair. It was a spring fantasy.

At the last minute, when Cee-cee had been stressing about crafting the perfect wedding cake after a long day of baking cupcakes for the shop, her sisters had taken over. She had been sent upstairs to her apartment for a good night's sleep, firmly instructed to stay out of the cupcake kitchen for the next two days. With Max's help, they had baked everything that the shop would need the day of her wedding *and* they had created a gorgeous, towering wedding cake made entirely of cupcakes.

Max, Steph, and Anna had taken Cee-cee's recipes, the ones they knew so well after countless hours of helping her in the shop, and put their own twist on each one. They had created a citrus wedding cake out of three different flavors: a base of Orange Creamsicle cupcakes drizzled with a Cointreau reduction, a middle layer of ginger-kumquat cupcakes with a limoncello glaze, and a top tier of vanilla cupcakes filled with lemon curd and topped with fluffy meringue. They were all phenomenal, each of them as good as anything that Cee-cee had ever made. Even better, because they had been made with such love.

The night flew by in a heady rush of joy, family, friends, and laughter. So many great moments would be forever etched in her mind — and the ones she forgot? Well, she'd have gobs of photographs.

Everyone got into the spirit of things, making good use of the disposable cameras that were scattered everywhere. Anna kept her camera in hand most of the night — though with an ever-present flute of champagne in her *other* hand, it was anybody's guess how many good pictures she would get.

Cee-cee didn't care. She didn't care if any of the pictures turned out. She'd print every one of them anyway, just for fun, but she didn't really need them. She would remember this night — and cherish it — for as long as she lived.

Grinning, Cee-cee wiped a speck of frosting from Mick's chin and pulled him back out onto the dance floor.

The evening was pure magic. And, later that night, after her wonderful husband had drifted off to sleep, his body curled protectively around hers, Cee-cee felt like the luckiest woman in the world. To have found such an amazing partner was an extraordinary gift in and of itself, but to have their union blessed by such a wonderful array of family? Cee-cee could hardly believe her luck. Her heart filled to bursting with joy and gratitude as she played the events of the day over and over in her head, thinking of how lovely it was to have Max and Gabe there to give her away.

She couldn't help but think of Patty Addison. How was it that some people had all of the luck and others had none? To have her two beautiful children taken from her... Cee-cee could hardly imagine the depth of the woman's grief. She supposed that being disconnected from reality was for the best in that situation.

At least there would finally be justice for Emily.

A shiver ran through her as she thought of Chaz

Bartholomew. It was so unsettling to learn that, all this time, there had been a killer living in Bluebird Bay. Eating at the diner. Shopping at the grocery store. It was hard to believe that someone who walked among them every day could have been responsible for such a heinous crime.

Cee-cee closed her eyes and tried to remember more about him. He and Nate had been buddies when they were in high school, but they'd drifted apart after Nate and Cee-cee had gotten together.

She had a vague memory of the last time she had seen him socially...she frowned as she dragged that day up from the depths of her memory, holding Mick's hand close to her chest to steady herself.

Barry had shown up to their house uninvited. It was a weekend night, and Cee-cee's whole family was there celebrating Mom's birthday. Even Anna, who was just starting out as a wildlife photographer, had made a point of coming home between trips for the big day.

Barry had knocked on the door and Nate answered. She remembered Nate inviting him in, but he'd looked around in surprise at the small crowd and declined, saying that he didn't mean to interrupt. Cee-cee remembered thinking it strange that he would show up out of the blue when Nate so rarely spoke to him.

Nate had offered him a drink and a piece of birthday cake, but Barry had left without coming in.

Something else, though...something about that night that had put Cee-cee on edge beneath the starched-shirt smile she always wore in those days. A short while after Barry had left, she'd been looking for Nate to get him to take out the overflowing trash. Anna had told her that he'd gone out to get more ice. Cee-cee remembered thinking it was strange, because they still *had* ice, but she'd written it off as him just trying to escape spending time with her family.

Nate was gone a long time, though. Nearly an hour. Long enough that her parents had gone home, and Cee-cee had started to worry. When he'd come back, he'd looked frazzled. She asked him what was wrong, and he told her that he'd run over a cat. She remembered thinking that was strange... he wasn't cruel to animals and loved dogs, but had no lost love for cats. Still, killing an animal *was* traumatic and Nate was visibly shaken, so she let him be and not thought of it again. She had a small son to care for and a second child who was just beginning to stir deep in her belly; she didn't have the time or the energy to mother her husband.

But now, in the dark of night, something pulled insistently at the corners of her mind.

With growing dread, Cee-cee slipped out of bed, sliding carefully out from under Mick's arm so as not to wake him. She walked into the kitchen and opened her laptop. The article about Emily Addison was in her recent search history, and she opened it back up. The girl was reported missing on December third... the first Saturday after Mom's birthday in November.

The day of the party.

The day that Emily's killer had shown up at their house, looking stressed and upset.

This realization hit Cee-cee like a blow to the head, and she snapped her computer shut.

Was it just a bizarre coincidence?

Or had her ex-husband, the father of her children, been

somehow involved in the disappearance and subsequent murder of Emily Addison?

Did you enjoy Finding Refuge? Check out Finding Comfort, coming in January!

Want more of the Sullivan sisters and the gorgeous coast of Maine right now? Check out the Cherry Blossom Point series in Starting From Scratch, out now and free with Kindle Unlimited!

A story of love, sisterhood, and starting over...
Lena Merrill and Owen McEnna have been best friends for decades, and she's done a great job of pretending she's not in love with him that whole time...until recently. Maybe it's all the changes in the air. Maybe it's realizing that life is passing her by and most of her dreams are still unfulfilled. Whatever the case, her already notoriously bad poker face is slipping, and it needs to stop, pronto. Because there's only one thing worse than not having Owen love her back, and that's the thought of driving him away altogether.

When Nikki Merrill set off for Bluebird Bay to find her long lost sister, Anna, she never imagined she'd be returning home to Cherry Blossom Point with her in tow. Battle lines are drawn when each of her siblings have wildly different reactions to their new family member. Lena is willing to invite Anna into their lives, Gayle and Jack can't even look at her, and Nikki? She's caught dead in the middle of things. Will building a relationship with her new sister splinter the one she has with the siblings she's always known?

Anna Sullivan didn't want another family. Now that she has one, though, she's in for the long haul. When she leaves Bluebird Bay to spend some time with Nikki and meet the rest of her siblings, she isn't prepared for the drama that ensues. It's kind of hard to make a good impression when half of them see her as a walking representation of their father's infidelity. And when more family secrets are uncovered, she realizes they've only seen the tip of the iceberg.

Will Anna figure out how to navigate these choppy family waters, or will her visit to Cherry Blossom Point turn out to be a disaster of Titanic proportions?

Get Starting From Scratch!

Want to get an alert next time a new book is out, find out about sales or contests, and chat with Christine? Join the mailing list **here!**

Maeve's Girls
(Standalone Women's Fiction)

Bluebird Bay
Finding Tomorrow
Finding Home
Finding Peace
Finding Forever
Finding Forgiveness
Finding Acceptance

Finding Redemption
Finding Refuge
Finding Comfort

Cherry Blossom Point
Starting From Scratch
Just Getting Started
A Fresh Start
A Head Start

Lucky Strickland Series (Mystery/Thriller)
Lucky Break
Getting Lucky

Crow's Feet Coven (Paranormal Women's Fiction)
Writing Wrongs
Brewing Trouble
Stealing Time

Made in United States
Troutdale, OR
03/03/2025

29445773R00134